THE **REPENTANCE**
of **LORRAINE**

ANDREI CODRESCU

THE REPENTANCE of LORRAINE

With a New Introduction by the Author
"Why I Did What I Did"

First Rhino*ceros* Edition 1993

First printing Septmber 1993

ISBN 1-56333-329-5

Cover Photograph © 1993 by Robert Chouraqui

Cover Design by Julie Miller

Manufactured in the United States of America
Published by Masquerade Books, Inc.
801 Second Avenue
New York, N.Y. 10017

WHY I DID WHAT I DID

I wrote *The Repentance of Lorraine* for money at the same time I was writing my autobiography *The Life and Times of an Involuntary Genius*. I was 23 years old, living in Monte Rio, California on about $300 a month in a perilously leaning shack over a ravine. I thought of my "autobiography" as "serious writing" and of *Lorraine* as an amusement, but the latter quickly became the part I was leaving out of my autobiography. The trouble with sex—which I was having plenty of in the lax days of 1973—was that it was a lot more anarchic (and fun) than typing. The difficulty was in finding the right tone, which lay neither in pornography nor in sentiment, but in the mystical. I felt that sex was transcendental, which is to say, untranslatable. What made the flesh rise was precisely what sank the page. My memory shaped experience to its own narrative exigencies, as well. That was plenty obvious in my autobiography where years and events telescoped for the sake of a paragraph as soon as I looked at a keyboard. And it was hard, to coin a phrase, to sit in my chair while the nude beach at the Russian River stretched tantalizingly just outside my picture window.

Nonetheless, I was trying to investigate, using sex, something beyond sex, namely the Mystery of Triangulation. No one had yet described to my satisfaction the intoxication and difficulties of a relationship between three people attempting to carry on the complexities of a triangle. Not that attempts hadn't been made. Literature was littered with the debris of threesomes, from the erudite speculations of Mircea Eliade in his journals and novels, to the domesticated novels of sentiment that populated the current shelves. The question had enthralled writers since the first narratives. A clever student could, I'm sure, make a case that the entire enterprise of literature was, in one way or another, an essay on the instability and desirability of the Triangle. The shape of three people loving and in love was both utopic and impossible. Of course, I didn't forget for a moment the money side of things so I tried to keep the surface readable if not actually light. It wouldn't have done, in this particular case, to apply the Sam Abrams porn-novel test of one erection per page, one climax per chapter, but I tried nonetheless to keep the readers' erectile needs in mind. After all, the all-too-real nut-brown bodies perking up outside, all nipples and hillocks on the beach, demanded a kind of veracity. Inevitably, the best girls, the baddest, would gather around a fire and a drum after dusk, passing the joints and the wine around, with Indian blankets over their shoulders against the chill but with breasts poling out and hair a big mess that just died to be firmly combed. So after the day's portion of Lorraine, I combed hair under the stars. Or maybe that was typing, too.

—Andrei Codrescu
New Orleans, May 1993

ONE

I don't want to give you any ideas in case you know Lorraine now. Just last week, she told me, two photographers wanted her to pose nude for a men's magazine, two sculptors wanted to look at her while they played with clay, one muralist wanted to put her on the wall of a synagogue, a famous visiting poet (another one) had some notion of writing his next poems on her body, and the ordinary mortals, if we are to speak of them, simply made her proposition after proposition. How in the world, you may ask, could such a demure, innocent girl attract such lavish attention? Such a demure, innocent, tastefully dressed girl who, in addition, is a serious business student at the University of Michigan?

I can tell you. She may go on forever refusing the attentions of the world, male and female, she may go on with her studies and be, someday, a stock analyst on Wall Street, she may even marry a good-looking executive and raise a family, she may even enter a nunnery if the world gets to be too much for her, but no matter what she'll do, there will always be a certain deliberateness in her innocence, a certain feigning in her demureness. And there will always be, just under the surface of that velvety skin, the possibility of erotic madness, a possibility which, in all modesty, was discovered by B. Stone (myself) and M. Kaminski, our friend.

Now when I see Lorraine we meet in safe places, in coffee shops on campus, and we talk to each other like sober relatives without ever breaking through the formal reserve which we set up for ourselves. The decision to play this particular game wasn't mine, just as it wasn't Myra's. It was Lorraine's and Lorraine's only. Lorraine has repented. Lorraine: this blue dress, these blue eyes, this fervent erotic imagination, these sparkling white teeth, especially this slim, nervous, beautiful body, this mixture of curiosity and religious notions, this wild child, this Lorraine is truly, unmistakably repentant. What have you done to her? you will ask, and I assure you we have done nothing except acknowledge what was there already, delight in it, set it free. If being free is a crime (and I know it isn't), then we are guilty, both Myra and I. But even Lorraine wouldn't suggest that.

We meet now, as I've said, in coffee houses, and we talk about small things. Sometimes Myra will join us. Our relationships aren't strained, just conventional, that's all.

The Wagon Wheel is a steak house, but the clientele is mostly students, so really it's a coffee house, that is, no one orders steak, just coffee and an occasional side of french fries. I am alone now, nursing a long cup of coffee, remembering another coffee house somewhere in Iowa when there were three of us sitting in a booth, not talking. The sun was turning cold, and big rain clouds were forming. There was no one else in the place except an old woman at the counter and a young waitress behind it. The old woman was talking to herself softly, and we were feeling good, the three of us, our bodies glowing confidently. Then suddenly the old woman screamed at the young waitress: "WHY DON'T GOD ORDAIN THINGS DIFFERENTLY?" and the young waitress continued polishing her long red fingernails, not moved to answer. She gave us a look like *"a lot of nuts come and go this way and they all say crazy things if only that worthless old man I got hustling out there on Portland would come back and get me—God I hate this job."* Her look was directed to us, but I could tell she lumped us with the nuts. We looked dirty, perverted, sexual; we looked also, I hope, enticing. I can't be sure, but I have a hunch that Lorraine's repentance began right then and there. We'd been on the road for months. Perhaps right then and there, at the end of summer, a long shiver went through Lorraine and she began her descent. I don't know. She had two choices: California and the sunshine or back to school. I had a feeling (nothing certain, mind you) it could have gone either way. What frightened Lorraine wasn't the love we showed her but the power she had over us, over Myra and me, a power almost absolute. Nowhere, beginning in her sheltered and peanut-buttered, softened childhood, continuing through her back-seat vinyl adolescence and girlish fantasies, had the seeds of such an idea been implanted except in the sense that it is human nature to desire infinite power, boundless beatitude. But when human nature is plied with devotion as lavish as ours, you get dangerously close to the absolute.

"Why did you quit your job?" Lorraine asked me, a few days after I'd taken that fatal wrong turn to the kitchen. We were in a coffee house on campus, it could have been the Wagon Wheel, and her question did not seem unnatural. She was squinting in her particular, sexy way, her big blue eyes looking a bit tired.

I made up this fantasy for her. I quit my job, I told her, to write a Great Story. This was the truth. I didn't mention the demise of my Aunt Dorothy, who left me, in her will, ten thousand big American dollars to spend as I saw fit. My Great Story, greatly supported by Aunt Dorothy's generosity, was going to be unlike any story ever written, an ambition which, I am sure, has occurred to many who have quit their jobs on the spur of the moment without saying good-bye to their fellow teachers or giving notice to their bosses. But there was, in all modesty, a difference between me and the others. As I then patiently explained to Lorraine, I wanted to write a story that was *alive*, in the manner of those old churches that have women built alive in their walls. I wanted to write a story in which a woman was contained. Totally. I wanted my words to take on the shape, the mind and the beauty of this woman. I wanted to write words that caressed like a passionate woman, words that moved as beautiful women move through doorways onto a chair, to a mirror, or in bed. I wanted words steeped in that moist darkness where we originate and where we return, over and over. It was natural then that I would need a model for my story just as a sculptor or a painter would. No fantasy woman could have done what a real one could.

Perceptively, Lorraine said: "And I'm on my way."

"There is Myra too, you know," I reminded her.

"Ah, but Myra loves *me*."

"Myra loves us both, in that order."

"Sounds dreadful," the child leapt back, "being trapped in a story."

"Or in a church, for that matter."

"Or in school or at home or in a police station."

"Or in a dream or in an ugly body or in a small brain."

"Or in now or in forever or in…."

We were warming up now, and Lorraine threw her legs over the side of the booth, not bothering to pull her mini down from the high place where her silk panties showed, and the Wagon Wheel began to spin. This was too beautifully spontaneous, so I burst out laughing. She was annoyed.

"Does the leg show bother you?"

Far from it, ladies and gentlemen. Lorraine was the owner of a sublime pair of legs. Walking places with her meant collecting the gazes of clerks, passers-by and all that can see.

"No, no," I said, "why should it bother me?"

This was only three days after the wrong turn to that strange kitchen in that strange house where it all began.

We all loved coffee (and cigarettes), Myra, Lorraine, and I, and all across the USA and in Europe we had thousands of cups of black coffee. The coffee I'm drinking now, by myself, tastes nothing like the espressos we had in Rome, listening to the jukebox on the sidewalk café, or even the cowboy coffee we had in Transylvania when we camped out and slept in one sleeping bag.

Lorraine put her calves back under the table. The Wagon Wheel stopped spinning.

"Where the hell is Myra?" she asked. "She always makes me wait."

Always! Three days ago, Myra had been a respected teacher to young frump here, and now it was already *she always*.... Three days ago we didn't even exist to each other.

I stroked her knee under the table. She shivered visibly. Her knee, encased in her silk stocking, grasped my hand if that is possible. I could feel it. With my hand, like this, on Lorraine's beautiful knee, I felt ready, in a thousand ways, to burst though my clothes like a hot spring.

My mind wandered slowly from her knee up toward some junction of her thighs where I imagined a sudden frill decorating the front of her silk panties with a beautiful arabesque line of love-wetness.

It took the knee that solicited this only a second to comprehend it. It took me only a second to communicate it. Lorraine was red from the tips of her ears to the tips of her toes, the Wagon Wheel was spinning again, and the table between us was melting without spilling the coffee.

"Let's get out of here," she whispered.

"But Myra ... She'll be mad if...."

But Lorraine was already coming gracefully toward me, and we disappeared on campus just as an April shower began to fall from the sky.

In her room at the dormitory Myra was waiting

for us. Before we even got in the door she said, "I wanted to know if you'd dare play without me. I guess you would, you little rats." Then she unfastened the sari she was wearing, with one hand. It swirled to the ground, and there was Myra, stark naked and beaming.

That was Myra. The same Myra who had been on the other side of that door, the wrong turn in that strange house.

TWO

Aunt Dorothy's money didn't come right away, there being a complicated will to probate, but the day I heard of my dear aunt's generosity I quit my job. My rent was paid up in advance for February, and I was stocked up on food for a couple of weeks at least. I had so looked forward to this time I didn't even get out of bed that day. I stood there watching the gorgeous clouds and dreaming of my newly found freedom.

Since December 1939, the month of my birth, I had done millions of stupid things punctured here and there by arrows of true pleasure. Through the holes these arrows tore in the dull material of my existence I could see tiny glimmers of light on the other side. My fantasies, based on these intimations, were fabulous. I can honestly say that I have never been poor,

17

although money was a matter of conjecture more than, let's say, the routine I follow. I have always imagined myself rich, beautiful and admired. The occasional flatteries a man will receive from occasional lovers became the solid base on which I made my pitch for a better life. I am not sure whether the decision to be a writer followed or preceded these fantasies. Some may have seen me as the typical schoolteacher who wrote poetry in his spare time as he walked down the street wrapped in a ridiculous black windbreaker which, together with the badly pressed beige pants, constituted this image of myself I fought against valiantly. And I admit I was fighting more often than not. But now I looked forward to Aunt Dorothy's money as a way out of this. I could write unbothered. Expectation was welling up inside me. I was alone and unattached, and I wanted to write a Great Story.

At this point in time, an image of Lorraine wearing her faded jeans and the T-shirt that says DRC (Dubuque Racquet Club) comes to mind. She is striding across the fields on Easter vacation under a sunset that thrills her, thinking of going back to school tomorrow, a faint excitement growing. It is cold, and her nipples are hard.

I, in my bed, am dreaming of the woman I will wall in in my story. I imagine her sophisticated, rich (like myself), flicking her ashes onto the carpet from her long cigarette holder, a woman of mysteries and curious tastes. In my imagining, I am the innocent one. Meanwhile, the real innocent one holds a half-eaten Mars Bar between her pensive fingers and declares to

Mom, Pop, little brother and Grampa: "I'm thinking of joining a sorority," a statement that thrills the assemblage but makes no sense, really. Sororities have gone the way of the twist, and Lorraine is a hip woman. But she has her moments. She likes to give hope.

The sophisticated woman, on the other hand, has just gotten out of bed, looked at her naked image in the mirror. She is satisfied by its taut youthfulness, happy that the kiddies are in school, that hubby won't be back for three days, and happy in general without knowing why. She sits cross-legged on her wide bed and opens a leather-bound diary in which she has been inscribing her intimate thoughts for a month or so. On the cover of the book, a gift from the professor, her name is engraved in raised gold letters: M-Y-R-A. She touches each letter of her name and smiles. Just a great day, that's all.

It is night when I finally leave my bed. My first day of freedom was a pleasure. I had not had to mold my dreams around the contours and conversations of my fellow commuters. Nor was I forced to steal time for reverie from classrooms, meetings and other obligations. I reviewed my life calmly and from an angle of expectant beauty. I would begin to write my story.

But first I had to borrow some money to get by until the will had cleared. I went through my telephone address book. Noticing how it was filled with the names of poor wretches who shopped at the Safeway just like me. They didn't have three hundred dollars between them. The only likely candidate in there was Ron Dreyfus, an old friend of mine who'd made it big in the antique auction business. He was a curious fellow; I hadn't seen him in years, but I remembered him as a man of black humor with a penchant for practical jokes. His becoming an auctioneer had been one of his whims because he had, as far as I know, a Ph.D. in English from Iowa. And a couple of years in Army Intelligence.

I called up Ron at the offices of Auction House Unlimited. He was working late, his answering service told me. In what I imagined to be the emptiness of a giant warehouse filled with the ghosts of outraged Biedermeier furniture, I heard my phone ring. Ron answered: "Joe's Bar and Grill!"

"Hi. Ron?"

"Cooking."

"This is your friend from the Middle Ages," I said.

He recognized me without trouble, and a cheerful note of suspicion as often is heard between sporadic friends crept into his voice:

"Come on over," he growled. "I'll show you to a Black Mass."

Black Mass, my ass. The guy was still insane.

I had some difficulty finding the warehouse, since there were thousands of railroad tracks in my way, and once I nearly drove into a locomotive parked in the shadows between two huge warehouses abandoned to the night. It was assuredly a spooky neighborhood. I've always gotten a spooky feeling from places that are full during the day and then empty at night, like bottles of ink.

"Hi," he said from someplace in the vast room after I had found the door.

At this time, Lorraine's already back on the night train that's taking her to Ann Arbor, safely ensconced in an empty first-class compartment, staring out the window at the startling ghosts of the electrical wires following the train into infinity. Her mind is at ease in the vastness of the night outside. She likes the movement and wishes it would never stop. Somewhere, out there, in the night, in the little villages glimpsed along the way, the people are dreaming. Lorraine is interested in dreams, she has always tried to interpret hers. She imagines herself walking unseen into the dreams of all the people, rearranging the scenery, whispering lines to the dream people, showing her sudden, naked body in the midst of a fire. Every village the train goes through experiences, in the course of that night, an epidemic of erotic dreaming, and it is a night remembered long after.

Myra is entertaining friends. Like Lorraine raping her sleepers, Myra devours her guests with her wit and her intelligence. Her conversation draws people the way one sees it in films. Or the way one thinks it could have been with Madame de Stael minus Benjamin Constant. She talks about the weather. Listen:

"Good thing about these tornadoes: They wake everybody up."

Interlocutor: "They need it at the university. Everybody's sleeping."

"I had a dream last night...."

There were no overstuffed chairs in sight, and Ron Dreyfus had aged. His hair was gray. He was affable.

"There are only two reasons any of our gang sees

me now: for money or for advice in business matters."

"Money," I said.

We went up to his office, which was a combination bedroom, kitchen and shower. The place was full of books and posters, and I stepped all over various diagrams and computer tear-outs.

"You want to have dinner here with a couple of girls?" he asked.

Certainly.

He made his phone call, during which he was rather businesslike and reserved.

"Monique and Colline, two French girls I met recently. They are beautiful. Monique is completely insane and does the most incredible burlesque. Colline is virginal, in that sexy French-nun way."

"Sounds great," I said. "What's for dinner?"

"Chinese. They'll cater here in an hour. Meanwhile, let's have some Scotch. Gotta get in the mood."

The stereo is tastefully loaded with some polite African rhythm. We sip our Scotch and talk about common memories.

Myra's husband, Dr. Kaminski, puts his hairy hand on the shoulder of a college professor dressed in a white pullover and pulls him toward the core of an argument on eroticism. Dr. Kaminski is an archaeologist. He is working on an understanding of the species from a moral angle. To this end, the professor has begun collecting ancient pornography and tracing curves between various historical peaks. The valleys between these peaks are occupied, the professor says, by settled people, agricultural people, land cultures. The peaks are inhabited by warriors, migrants, drifters. War, blood and violence reign at the tips, while peace and prosperity blossom in the valleys.

Lorraine arrives in Ann Arbor at 4:30 in the morning. She pulls her dreamy suitcase up the path toward the university, hoping for a cab. Two lonely cars whoosh through the bluish night. It's cold, and she feels suddenly enormously tired as she trudges up the hill to Hill Street.

Colline was truly beautiful, and Monique was truly insane.

Lorraine has reached her dormitory. Wearily, she drags out the key to her room, crawls into her bed in the dark and screams. There is someone in her bed. The light is turned on, and the terrified freshman in pajamas tries to explain as he turns white that he thought nobody would be in the dormitory for three days yet and he is sorry oh so sorry he'll get up in one minute and leave and pray don't call the desk. Lorraine's maternal instincts are aroused.

"Stay where you are," she says wearily and begins to take off her clothes while the petrified freshman sits there paralyzed.

The guests have all gone home, Myra pulls her husband into the bedroom. He's in a grumpy mood.

"They think I'm an old pervert," he mutters.

"Aren't you?" she asks, touching his back as they sit on the bed to disrobe.

"No, dammit! I'm a serious scientist interested in the *wisdom* of pornography."

"It's the details that get me," she says, stretching full length.

The Professor laughs and, condescendingly, leans down and places a smug kiss on her navel. Then he turns over and begins dreaming, immediately, of an Etruscan cockfight. As for Myra, she stands there for a few seconds, her finger pensively poised at the entrance to the boat, decides against it, turns over and enters directly into contact with Lorraine, who is unknown to her but thrilling nevertheless.

Next morning I had my three hundred dollars, the memory of a giddy night full of antics and antiques, I felt good and free and I began to plan my little trip. Ron, who knows these things, told me to look up an old friend of his, a professor at the University of Michigan who could help my writing by introducing me to various writers he knows. Dr. Kaminski, his friend, is extremely hospitable and is, besides, a tremendous scholar, an archaeologist and a medieval historian.

I flew there, next day.

On her first day in school, Lorraine threw out the freshman and told him not to show his face in her room again or she'd report him for rape. Then she crumpled up the sheets on her bed and went to the laundromat, where she stood until the laundry was dry, reading the notices tacked on the wall. One of these captured her attention:

SECRETARIAL HELP NEEDED.
INQUIRE IN THE HISTORY DEPARTMENT

"Yes," they told her at the desk, "Dr. Kaminski needs a girl for some typing, some research and running some errands."

Professor Kaminski amused her the minute she saw him. He was a pipe-smoking professor full of imaginary authority. It amused her even more when the good doctor told her frankly that certain areas of his research might be bothersome to her and that if she was in the least shocked she ought to tell him right there and then so they wouldn't run into problems later.

"Shocked by what, Professor?" she asked.

"Sex," he said, taking a deliberate puff on his pipe and looking her squarely in the eyes.

"You and me?"

"No, no, sex in art and religion." Professor Kaminski looked relieved.

His relief shocked Lorraine, who said, "Oh!" in a truly shocked way.

But she had not been shocked by the doctor's remark. No, it was the calendar over his desk. Apparently religious, this calendar, on closer look, was misleading. Close up, the picture of St. George slaying the dragon was composed of thousands of miniatures. His halo, his lance, as well as his pontifically skinny body, accommodated hundreds of miniaturized nymphs and cherubs playing out an intense sexual drama. Lorraine suspected the calendar to be only the beginning of many things that were not what they seemed. She was right.

The professor studied her gaze. "That," he said, "is one of the many creations of a secret love cult of the seventeenth century. Look at this...." He held a crystal paper-holder for her inspection.

Gingerly, Lorraine grasped the object and gasped when she saw what floated there. Sixteen delicately drawn pubescent girls danced on a jet of spray issuing from a demonically laughing Cyclops.

At the professor's home, Myra holds an identical crystal paper-holder. She has looked at it thousands of times, and each time it has looked exquisitely rich. She loves it.

Which is the same minute, I believe, that I take my suitcase from the taxi and enter Ann Arbor, looking for a coffee house.

THREE

Whenever in doubt, see if the sun is shining. It was. I was sipping my coffee slowly, enjoying its hot black presence, enjoying also the noisy, scattered atmosphere of the Wagon Wheel: the students running to and fro with their bundles of books, the spaced-out characters leaning back behind their shades, the whole bright feeling of Ann Arbor that morning, and the incredible sign over the coffee machine: refills free. I could look forward to writing my Great Story here. Already, the women I saw looked freer and better than they had back home. Long-legged Eastern girls walked energetically across the sidewalk, in and out of shops, bookstores and coffee houses. A few years ago I had made my living traveling to various college campuses in California to read my poetry. These readings had given me a great number of opportunities for casual sex, and I had obliged the mythic image of poet by appearing as promiscuous as possible. I also indulged, of course. But things were different now. I wasn't looking for quantity, not as I had when I wrote that poem beginning Sex: *Is it a matter for poetry or just another notch on the gun?* No, I wasn't asking that kind of question any longer. I was looking for ecstasy, for a living model to wall into my Great Story. I had the time, all the time in the world, and soon I would have the money.

As I sipped my coffee, Myra sat back on her bed (still a couple of hours before the kiddies got home from school) and began to write in her diary:

Some people see religious figures in the snow, while others see sex in it. I belong to the latter category. All winter I've been in a state. I also see sex in the joining windows, in the archways of doors, on the pattern a fence makes on the ground, in shadows. Who is to say those myriad of angles we see every day are not joined sexually?

I finished my coffee and, leaving my suitcase under the table, I got up to call Dr. Kaminski.

"The professor won't be back until the afternoon," Myra said. "Can I take a message?"

"My name is Brandon Stone, I am a friend of Ron Dreyfus from San Francisco."

"I will tell him. Staying long, Mr. Stone?"

"I don't know yet," I replied. "I'm working on a story."

"You are a writer? A number of our friends are writers," she said. "Why don't you come here around seven? We are having a small, intimate party. Some of them will be here."

"Thank you, Mrs. Kaminski. I look forward to meeting you."

"Good-bye, Mr. Stone."

"Good-bye, Mrs. Kaminski."

I was standing, center stage, in a pleasant living room, large by my standards, pleasantly dimmed. A number of people, obviously familiar with each other, reclined comfortably on couches and chairs, watching the logs burning in the fireplace or talking amiably.

"A drink?"

"Scotch, please."

Mrs. Kaminski, my hostess, was wearing a long, clinging dress which set her body in a beautiful light as she strode away to get my drink. Professor Kaminski approached.

"I would like you to meet Dr. Müller," he said. "Dr. Müller is a biologist and, I should add, a very skeptical man. He does not believe in free will. Pornography, he maintains, is the work of a few stray cells without much say at the basic levels."

"It's the work of the devil, if I may say so myself," a short, dark, squat man interpolated, pushing his cigarette dramatically forward.

Dr. Kaminski and Dr. Müller smiled in unison, an indulgent smile which I have had the occasion to witness on many an academic lip.

"This is Victor Torso, poet and critic," said Dr. Kaminski.

"This is Brandon Stone looking for a story in Ann Arbor."

"The only story you'll find here, Brandon, is a persistent hangover. It began with the presidency of Dr. Clark. There is nothing real here. It's full of young idiots and old bores."

"My story, Mr. Torso, has nothing to do with reality. It's going to be more of a bear trap than a story."

"Hmmm." Torso pulled me aside as Kaminski continued to Müller: "I am sure that a perfect Renaissance man has created this particular object...."

"Nonsense," said Dr. Müller. "A Renaissance mind does not synthesize pornography on principle...."

"What do you mean?" asked Torso impatiently.

"I want to catch a live woman," I said, "and make my words take on her flesh and her personality. It's like an intricate cage, this story...."

"Did you find a rat for this experiment yet?" He didn't wait for a reply. "Don't get me wrong, friend, but it doesn't sound that original. It's what writers have done to their unfortunate spouses and girlfriends since the beginning of time. That's why they have rotten reputations."

With my drink in her hand, Mrs. Kaminski said: "Who has a rotten reputation?"

I took my drink from her hand and smiled.

"Writers," said Torso, giving Myra a look of infinite lust and malevolence. "I wouldn't be surprised if Doc's new obsession wasn't *your* idea...."

"Without his reasons, of course." Myra smiled.

And with this smile began my long journey into the night because I found myself, suddenly, without warning, totally enveloped by this woman's presence. I found myself completely absorbed, captivated, alas, gagged and bound to her smile. She exuded sexuality and mystery like an oriental stage set. "Is that true?" I managed to mumble with that naiveté which is the beginning of true love. Naiveté like speechlessness, accompanies love, walks before it like a knight. Even Torso recognized the symptom.

"Myra is a very dangerous women," he said. "It will be you in that cage...."

The charm did not subside later when, the party almost over, Mrs. Kaminski and myself, occupying a small corner of the couch, talked to each other of the subtleties of sex. Our conversation, flowing, as it were, out of the closeness of our bodies, was as natural as a brook, crystal clear to both of us. We could have been exchanging Greyhound schedules with the same intensity, however. We could have just sat there too, for that matter, wordlessly. From one thing to another our conversation skidded flawlessly, attaining at times masterful levels of Huysmanesque non sequitur. I found out, incidentally, what Dr. Kaminski's obsession was, namely, a fantastic object, a kind of cup or chalice which he had deduced exists hidden somewhere. This chalice was said to be the creation of a certain Renaissance genius who, in building it, had taken it on himself to synthesize the world's wealth of erotic pictures and had ended thereby creating the world's most comprehensive anthology of dirty delights, all set magnificently in gold and precious stones. There was no documentary evidence that this chalice existed besides Dr. Kaminski's postulation of it.

"It is the sole key to my theory," Kaminski himself said later. "If I can find it, I can change all current thinking on the matter."

Myra and I hadn't even gotten as close as an inch if you're looking at the sofa, but inside us the positions of our bodies toward each other can be seen reflected on the side of the professor's chalice. We were as close as two bodies can safely be without having to call the man with the saw. Without looking at her I knew that Myra's body was whole, there was precise synch between her long fingers and her smile, between her hair and her beautiful oblong face. I was magnetized. I tried to sober up for an instant by envisioning this woman as the head of a cult which demands in routine payment the blood of a poet. It didn't work.

Dr. Kaminski pushed his last guest out with a frown and a grunt and came toward us.

The shock was comparable to a sudden gush of red paint out of your favorite transistor radio. It was excruciating.

"Have you made arrangements for a place to stay, Mr. Stone?" he said, oblivious.

Yes, I had. I certainly had. I was going to stay exactly where I was.

He took a puff from his pipe. "We have a guest room that you are welcome to use tonight. Perhaps now that all the others have gone we could have an unencumbered intelligent talk."

And the good Dr. K began to talk. With each word he snipped a tiny thread from the vast network of luminescent fibers going from me to Myra and vice versa.

When Myra and I were finally separated, like Siamese detached twins, we stood for another minute in complete anesthetic shock and then rose to go to bed. Which goes to show how an aesthetic can turn into an anesthetic.

My room was at the end of a hallway, and long after I heard the hosts' bedroom door snap shut I felt that velvety figure attached like a yo-yo to my heart.

I could not sleep. The strange woman breathing in one of the rooms of the strange house hovered in the air above me. We were listening to each other through the walls.

Since she was listening and I in my head was talking, I told her the comic book version of my love life:

"At ten I presented an elaborately drawn Batman to a fifteen-year-old girl. She reciprocated by pretending to drop her slip accidentally one day and showing me a dazzling image of her body. At twelve I asked her for an explicit repetition of her action, but she laughed and asked: 'Where is my Batman?' From twelve to fifteen I drew endless sheaves of increasingly complex Batmen which I stashed in drawers, not having the courage to show them to her. I did show them to her much later, when she was married to a navy captain and we had an affair. But during those years there had been other girls. Would you like a picture, Myra?"

"I just wanna boogie," she said in her dream to little Lorraine, who pulled up her stocking.

I can't say it was a dreamless night, but of the dreams of lust I will say nothing. There is nothing new under the sun, the psalmist is only going through the motions.

Soon it was morning, and I woke at once. But I didn't recognize the room where I was lying.

I opened the door and found myself in a hall flooded with light from three different skylights. I kept walking down this hall, still drowsy and trembling slightly as I do before my first cup of coffee, and then I pushed open the door that I thought led to the goddamned kitchen but which led, instead, to the present farrago.

The room was a bedroom, and sprawled across the king-size bed, the naked beauty who had, last night, plugged me full of arrows was doing a set of exercises which involved pulling one leg and then the other up as far above the head as possible, thereby offering me a plentiful view.

I stood there with my hands in the pockets of the gown I had borrowed from the professor, looking incredulously at my luck.

"Pardon me," I said.

She sprung up in a lotus position and faced me without surprise, embarrassment, etc., only a complete self-awareness through which I was compelled to see just how perfectly full and firm her breasts stood behind the hard nipples, just how wild yet elegant her auburn pubic triangle reflected in the sunlight.

"Did you sleep well?" she asked.

I was still standing in the doorway, still looking at her nude outlines, the way her abundant blond-red hair fell over one shoulder.

"That damn bed had a pea in it," I answered.

"Sit down. I'll go get some coffee."

There was no place to sit except on the bed, so I approached cautiously and balanced on the edge. She got up and put on a loose robe. The buttons and hoops were missing, revealing more than the usual amount of safe-professor's-wife cleavage. Then she left me alone.

The bedroom was like a thousand others. There

were the pictures of the two daughters from year one; the little bookshelf filled with yoga, diet and Japanese erotic art; mauve curtains; the inevitable oblong mirror, antiqued around the edges; the half-open bottom drawer with silk stockings spilling over the edge; and the open closet door with the outlines of a well-caressed wardrobe glowing darkly. In fact, the only unusual feature was the bed I was sitting on, of truly magnificent size, spanning the width of the room like a stage or a command post. The rumpled sheets seemed to be satin. I slipped my hand under the blanket where the woman had just been. Yes, they were satin, and they were still warm.

"Feeling my bed?"

"Yes," I said. She was standing in the doorway.

"Well, feel," she said. "The coffee will be done in just a moment." Then she joined me on the bed. Sitting cross-legged, facing me, she reached for a cigarette on the nightstand and lit it. "Hmmm," she said, "this is freedom. The girls are in school, the husband is in school, the neighbors are in school...."

"And the sun is out," I said, still feeling the sheet between us with my outstretched palms.

"What are you doing?"

"Feeling the space between us," I said rather truthfully.

"A lot of work," she said and tossed her head back to watch.

I ventured to put my hand on her knee, and there it remained. Her big green eyes followed a straight line down the front of my robe. "You look terrible in the professor's clothes," she said.

The parts of my body involved in the above scene were as follows: the pit of my stomach, whence a sweet whirl of energy issued savagely; my heart, which was accelerating; and my entire genital apparatus, which began a vast blood transfusion, rendering the front of my robe into a flag.

"Quiet," she said, this time speaking directly to my cock as if it were a separate entity. "You may have to wait."

I couldn't; I slid toward her and took her in my arms. But a flourish of her hand indicated the coffee must be ready, and she rose gracefully, swinging her legs in one motion onto the floor.

I have been treated with hesitation before, but Myra wasn't just hesitating. She was playing a very subtle game which might, like imaginary undressing, take several days.

When she returned, she was balancing a tray full of coffee cups, sugar, milk and spoons. She sat next to me, our thighs touching, and put the tray across both of our laps.

This scene, you will notice, recurs systematically during our acquaintance. There we are, in a hotel on Via Degli Giardini Giovanni in Rome, balancing a tray full of coffee across our three laps, Myra in the middle, Lorraine and I on either side of her. Our thighs (naked) are touching, the summer breeze is rustling the curtains (open windows) and outside, the sexy noises of Rome. Or in Paris, on a train going to Aix-en-Provence, just before or shortly after we leave the station: coffee on our laps, thighs are touching (jeans and jeans and jeans).

"What do you take?"

"I'll have it black, thank you." I lifted my cup, and the warmth that hit my face combined with Myra's warmth. We were so close I could smell her very subtle perfume. She smelled like a dream animal and looked at me over the edge of her raised coffee cup with her animal eyes. Suddenly the tray, nudged on by my hardening member, began to tilt at a dangerous angle.

She grabbed a hold of it just in time and started to laugh. Then she slipped her right hand underneath and, finding an opening in my robe, she took hold of my rudder, pushing it down until the tray was, once again, even. Her index finger slowly caressed its tip. My hard cock rose from her hand like the pistil of an exotic flower. We put the tray on the floor. I unbuttoned the top of her loose garment, and her beautiful breasts bounded into view, her nipples sublimely erect. It is unfortunate, but nature has decreed that one breast must be chosen first over the other. I chose the left. Beginning at the outermost edge, my tongue climbed toward the pink aureole in the middle of which the nipple rose. A flicker of my tongue would set this sheikhdom on fire. But she stopped me. I looked at her questioningly.

"I want you to look at me fully," she said. "I like to be admired. I'm an exhibitionist."

She let the robe fall from her shoulder in a graceful and authoritative gesture and stretched her full naked length on the bed. Her hand rested lightly on my erection.

The doorbell could have been ringing for hours for all I knew. But worse, a young blonde picture of shock and dismay was standing on the doorway, one fist raised as if still bent on knocking though the time for that had passed. She stood rooted there with her eyes fixed on us. Her blush and breathlessness turned suddenly to a crimson flush of excitement, and her lips seemed to receive a new redness.

"Who are you?" Myra asked, which surprised me. I fully expected this was mama's little darling home early from school.

"I'm sorry...." she said, "I didn't know ... I knocked.... My name is Lorraine ... Dr. Kaminski's new assistant.... He sent me to get him the stack on fellatio ..." and, realizing what she'd just said, she blushed even more deeply.

"His stack on fellatio?!" asked my hostess absent-mindedly.

"The whole stack?" I said.

"Lorraine, come here."

The girl approached Myra with faltering steps.

"I have daughters your age," Myra said.

This fact seemed to calm the palpitant young creature, who now sat boldly on the edge of the bed, her arms crossed demurely in front of her.

"You must be a virgin," Myra said. "Don't be afraid. It's only a cock." Myra nodded toward my rigid organ, which independently started a brand new ascent to power.

"I know," whispered Lorraine, "I've seen...!" She stopped abruptly.

"Go on, touch it, don't be afraid. He wants you to touch it...."

Dreamily the girl extended her hand and brushed lightly against me with her fingers.

"Lorraine," said Mrs. Kaminski sternly, "take it in your hand...."

It is here that a certain pattern may have been fixed. The stern mistress telling the young boarding-school intern to bare her ass!

Lorraine did as she was told, getting a good grip.

Myra stood up on her knees and, embracing Lorraine gently from behind, deftly lifted her sweater up to her arms, revealing two young breasts tightly squeezed in by a pink bra. (This is the last we see of this bra.) She unfastened the pink strap, and the girl's breasts swung free. Cupping them lightly with her hands, Myra began to massage them, expertly exciting the nipples, which now stood like raisins on cupcakes. Lorraine's grip on my cock tightened.

"Stand a little," Myra urged Lorraine, pulling at her short skirt, which she had already unzipped in the back.

Lorraine stood gracefully, and her skirt slid down her legs to her ankles. Her young ass, enclosed by a pair of silk panties, had the forward freshness of brand-new cantaloupes.

Myra lifted the girl in her arms and put her on the bed. Lorraine still held on to my cock, which seemed to have become her rudder in the unexpected storm that had broken over her. Myra pulled the girl's sweater over her head, slipped down her panties. A vision of pubescence greeted us as the tiny patch of blond hair covering the fairly prominent mound of Venus began to glisten with beads of sweat.

"Lorraine would like you to pleasure her," Mrs. Kaminski said to me. "Wouldn't you, Lorraine?"

Lorraine looked at the older woman confidingly. "I like him," she said.

I was surprised, as we had only just met, but my member rewarded her by bobbing in her hand. I was burning and melting.

"He likes you, too," our hostess said. "See?"

Then Lorraine did a curious thing. She asked if Myra would stay.

How could we refuse? There were no secrets among us. And besides, she was little more than a child. Her innocence was so sincere, her youthful eagerness accompanied by youthful fear, the kind that is so easily relieved by a mother's presence. So I took her, and all the while Myra sat by.

After a long silence filled with half-dreams, Myra said, "It's his car." She meant Dr. Kaminski.

I rose to my wobbly legs and, pulling the robe around myself, I went to the bathroom to pee.

Professor Kaminski came in screaming, "Where is my fellatio stack?" Then, seeing me, he said, "Ah, there you are, my dear fellow." He carefully stroked his carefully combed Vandyke. "I know poets get up late.... You are night birds all, aren't you?"

I conceded easily.

Then I said, "This morning I sensed I could write my story here. There is something in the atmosphere, a creative attribute...."

This was devilish, I admit, but completely spontaneous. You see, I had realized there would not be one but *two* women encased in my Great Story.

"Dear fellow," Kaminski exclaimed, "of course. You are welcome to spend a few more days here. I am sure my wife will be delighted! We have so many things to talk about. Do you play chess?"

"I'm afraid not."

"Well, well, all the same, you are welcome. You can also speak to my class if you feel up to it. You can tell them anything.... They are green."

"Myra!" he shouted. "Myra, where are you? And where is my goddamn fellatio stack?"

"I'm showing Lorraine some new exercises," a voice came from somewhere in the house.

"Mr. Stone decided to stay a few days longer," he shouted back.

There was silence. Then a calm voice answered, "I hope he likes my cooking."

FOUR

The kid Lorraine had thrown out of her room two days ago was in the class I was lecturing to. I didn't know this at the time, but he was obviously a freshman and this was a graduate class. He sneaked in, probably thinking he'd see pornographic slides. He glared at me the entire time I spoke.

This was Professor Kaminski's pet class, The Curve of Pornography, history for graduate students. It amazed me to see these otherwise good-looking young people clutching notebooks in which the phallic statues of the Romans were explained as *the impulse, ritualized, by which the Roman armies achieved control of the entire oval of the Mediterranean.* Through these bound notebooks the cocaine chuckles of Dr. Freud echoed derisively.

But I wasn't dismayed, since the subject of my

talk was literature and everyone knows what a genital mess that is. I had prepared a few notes but quickly abandoned them and began to freely improvise.

In the course of my lecture, I could barely hear the tiny voice commenting (perhaps) as I spoke. I strained to see its origin and was confronted by a perfect Lolita, bobby sox and all, an *affected* Lolita, I might add, since she must have been at least eighteen to be in school at all. But I wasn't sure: the girlish face, the pigtails....

"You are a writer," she said. "What percentage of your work is pornography and what percentage of that is peak or valley?"

My work is all pornography, and it's all peak, and I don't even write ... I would have liked to say, but instead I laid it on thick:

"I want to say that I conceive of fiction as an intricately built cage to hold a living person in it, a person so...."

"A female ... person?" Lolita asked.

"Well...."

After class Lolita stayed to ask some questions, and this is when Lorraine appeared with a bundle of books under her arm, looking regal. She swept into the classroom as everyone was filing out. I was asking Lolita, "How old are you?" and, from behind her, Lorraine answered, "She couldn't be older than I was yesterday."

The frosh stood next to me. He glared at Lorraine, who ignored him as she took my arm, from which she hung limply and obviously bored.

"She's right," said Lolita, giving Lorraine an innocent smile of sympathy.

"I can't stand that man," said Lorraine, pointing to the kid.

"You bitch!" the kid said.

Lorraine looked up at me with her nose, thus calling upon my chivalry.

I pointed at Lolita and said to the kid, "Mind your manners, there is a young girl here."

"Your first girl?" said Lolita to the kid, pointing at Lorraine.

"It's none of your business...." he said, blushing.

"How many times?"

"Once," Lorraine answered obligingly.

"IT'S NONE OF ANYBODY'S GODDAMNED BUSINESS!" raved the kid, taking the position sanctioned in his neighborhood as the Official Fight Pose.

Lolita squared off in front of him and said, "I can't believe my eyes! You're such a trip!"

They began fiercely eyeballing each other, determined not to blink until death, at which point Lorraine and I stepped aside and left. We headed for the Wagon Wheel and a cup of spin.

This is when Lorraine threw her legs in the air after asking me why I had quit my job and, hand in hand, we walked back to her dormitory, where Myra was waiting for us.

This second meeting between us was as qualitatively different from the one at the Kaminski house as day is from night, if you like night as I do. We three deeply explored each other: the miner with his lamp climbing into the bowels of the earth to hit a filon of gold, the hungry czar after the hunt, the whip gone insane on the flesh which it commands to open.... The frenzy of a bacchanalia seized us. We made love to each other in a timeless furor. This prolonged activity (it was midnight when we finally stopped to order a pizza) brought to the surface the amazing fact of our absolute compatibility. We fit into each other like a three-way lock. Our pleasures fitted together at their jagged edges as described by the Continental Drift Theory.

Due to this, an unknown freedom surfaced in me. My suppressed dramatic talents came to the surface with a bouquet of three-way plays, including this one in which:

The inverse V of Lorraine's nervous and pretty legs holds the globe of Lorraine's head like an offering from the inverse V of her legs (picture available; send $.50 to the author, c/o the publisher). And all this abandon, these gymnastics, this vision is taking place in a room the size of this desk, a room so tiny the bed does not fit—it has to be folded into the wall at an angle.

The pizza took nearly three-quarters of an hour. Lorraine went to open the door in the nude, thinking, I suppose, about the possibilities of the delivery boy.

The kid stood there in a not-so-white apron, holding a big square box. Upon seeing Lorraine his color deserted him.

"What's the matter?" said Myra and got up to see.

"Mrs. Kaminski ... gasped the boy, who recognized the professor's wife.

To add to the confusion I rose too and looked.

"Mr. Stone!"

To his credit, he didn't drop the pizza.

"I see you got a job," said Lorraine with new respect in her voice.

"That will be four-fifty," he said, giving her the pizza.

I was worried for Myra. It was already midnight, and the kid had recognized her. I didn't know what kind of arrangement she had with the professor, but whatever it was, the circumstances were not auspicious.

"Come in," ordered Lorraine.

Hypnotized, the white ghost of bygone youth entered the room as if stepping on a dream roof.

"I'll walk you home, Myra," I said.

She pouted, her eyes, lit by new visions, fastened on the frosh. She exchanged a quick smile with Lorraine, two young lionesses out for a kill.

"I'll walk you home, Myra," I repeated.

"Oh, well," she said and began to pick her scattered vestments from the assorted pile on the floor. It was cold outside, so she borrowed Lorraine's sweater to put over her sari.

We said good-night. But when we closed the door behind us, Myra turned to me and said, "I want to be back in there."

This I could not allow, but if you are hastening to look at my action as the onset of jealousy you couldn't be more wrong. As our stay together amply demonstrated, I could not be jealous of my two loves. I had no right to and had not the slightest inclination. Anything that made them happy was okay with me. I needed them for my story, that's all. I didn't want wives. But I couldn't stand the kid. I honestly felt like strangling him. Never in my memory of my youth have I ever seen such a helpless wreck, such a sniveling little…. I'm getting worked up because this kid has further occasions to outrage me during this story…. He's even got the gall, now that Lorraine has repented, to court her as if none of this had ever happened. I think he's planning to marry her! That little snort....

But enough. As I walked Myra home, arm in arm, it was so cold, I felt tired and the night was so dark, it seemed to me the two of us were the last people on earth, trudging on through the mud. We were filled, however, with the silver sparks of a deep satisfaction. Our bodies glowed.

At the professor's house the lights also glowed. A few of the friends were over. Victor Torso leapt at us from behind the fireplace.

"Aha! I see Myra's joined a sorority." She was wearing Lorraine's sweater with Greek letters on it.

"Oh, this," laughed Myra, and without so much as a glance to her guests she bounded upstairs.

Torso studied me. "You look—ahem—well fucked," he said.

"Excuse me, Victor, it was only a lecture I gave this morning in Doc Kaminski's class."

"Ah! The famous lecture by a visiting writer!"

Kaminski approached. "Thanks so kindly for bringing Myra home. These modeling classes run so late, I'm always afraid she'll be molested in the dark. She really should learn how to drive."

"She doesn't drive?" V. Torso feigned astonishment.

"Congratulations, by the way. The students told me it was a splendid lecture. I hope you're able to repeat the gist of it for me. I'm sorry the conference took so long. It's been a day of misses. Even my new assistant didn't show up for work, and I had to index a whole box of notes myself. Wasted time."

"I'm afraid your wife got her away from you," I said, before knowing what came out of my mouth.

"Really?" quipped Torso. "Interesting!"

"What I mean is … Mrs. Kaminski had some library work and Lorraine helped her."

"Ah," said the professor thoughtfully (puff on the pipe).

Victor: "A harrowing day."

Professor (to me): "There is someone I would like you to meet." We walked toward a tall, metaphysical blond in a Cardin suit. "This is Dr. Collins, the head of our department. Dr. Collins, Mr. Stone, a writer."

Dr. Collins began. It seemed the department had fifty thousand loose dollars, a grant from an anonymous donor. These dollars were still loose because it was hard to fulfill the condition of the grant, which was "toward work in the area of creative writing concerned with the influence of literature on its own characters." For example, what happened to Daisy Miller after reading James? (This list, of course, disregards the fact that those authors, in the interest of neatness, killed off their characters.)

Not believing my luck, in words carefully constructed to fulfill the conditions of the grant, I explained the idea behind my Great Story. Dr. Collins was impressed.

"Any friend of Dr. Kaminski's," he said, "qualifies for serious consideration."

We planned to meet in his office next day at noon. Then I went to bed, leaving Torso to sort out all the innuendos.

Next day, at the Wagon Wheel, I sipped my coffee, so happy with life. The sun was out and I was on my way to see Dr. Collins.

Myra had gotten up late that day. The professor

had no classes. I had not yet seen the couple's daughters except in photographs. They woke and went to bed too early for me. I had walked out of the house through the back door that morning, seeing no one.

Lorraine had gone to Kaminski's office, where she received orders by telephone to type up the longhand lists on her desk. Adjusting her secretarial gear about her, blinking wearily, Lorraine set herself to the task.

After breakfast, Myra went back to her bedroom, took down her diary and wrote:

I haven't been fucked like this in six years, almost to the date since my affair with M & B. In one respect, I have not been educated in vain. I am medieval like my hubby's prints. I believe in rules. I like to violate them.

Lolita walked into the Wagon Wheel just as I was about to leave for Dr. Collins' office.

"Hi," she said matter-of-factly, throwing her books on the table.

"I have an appointment. I have to rush. How did your battle with the kid turn out?"

"I had to fuck him," she said. "The only way to calm him down."

"That kid's getting a lot these days."

"I felt sorry for him."

"Look, I gotta go. See you later."

"Do you know where I can get a job?" she shouted after me.

In a nursery, I thought.

Dr. Collins wasn't in. I had to wait for a few moments. Looking at the clustered bookshelves of this academic man, I felt again the irony of my position; I had, only a few days ago, been a miserable high-school teacher with an efficiency apartment. And now, loaded with money I hadn't yet received, I was applying for a fifty-thousand-dollar grant to write what I was going to write anyway. "You lucky dog," I said.

"Yes," smiled Collins, unoffended, "I have a good life!"

"Professor! I didn't hear you come in!"

"It's the doors," he said. "I had them oiled. Like the couch. Have a seat."

I sank into a leather armchair.

"There is another angle to this grant," he said. "It's confidential. You know, of course, the thrust of Dr. Kaminski's theory."

"That there is a chalice or a cup someplace...."

"Yes."

" ... that synthesizes...."

"We can't run this department without him. But he needs to find this object. He is reasonably sure that hidden among the great European collections of erotica there is this overlooked masterpiece. Since we cannot send him abroad and his sabbatical isn't coming up for another year, I would like to send someone to find this essential object in the context of the grant."

"You would like me," I said, "if I qualify, to track down a chalice?"

"As well as," he continued, "to view, describe and analyze significant but little-known objects in the collections you are going to view."

"It sounds very cloak and dagger," I said.

"Not at all. We would like to be discreet about it, of course. Many of the collections we will ask you to view are well-known and accessible. Some, like Pompeii, need not even be seen. We have all those frescoes. But there are private collections in Rome, Paris and Eastern Europe which are not open to academic scrutiny. An individual, a writer like yourself, has a good chance though."

"How would such an object end up in a communist country?"

"Ah!" laughed Collins. "It might not be a Renaissance chalice. It could be Dacian, Thracian or Ugric. I disagree with Kaminski on that."

"Alone?" I said.

"I would imagine," the impeccable professor smiled, "that the grant is ample enough to warrant your hiring an assistant." He half-closed his eyes.

Visions of Lorraine following me through caves made me giddy.

"As a matter of fact," Collins said, "we have already found an assistant for you, if you care to trust me."

"Who?"

"Dr. Kaminski."

"But I thought he had to stay here…. The department, etcetera…."

"Not *he* …" countered Collins. "Dr. Kaminski's wife is also Dr. Kaminski…. She is a great European scholar…. "

"But … she has children, no?"

I don't know why I had to object. Perhaps to defend some semblance of normalcy. "It would seem highly incongruous…. I mean, Myra, I mean Dr. Kaminski and myself, you know…."

"She is a serious scholar, Mr. Stone, and her help would be invaluable to you."

Remarkable.

Later, I sat in the Wagon Wheel trying to connect my thoughts. This adventure seemed to have already been plotted out but had remained potential until I had shown up to fit into it like the missing puzzle piece. Whatever it is, I thought, what's the harm in it if it is exactly what I want to do? I suspected some kind of plot but a kind of plot I would generously abandon myself to. Myra Kaminski was going to be my assistant. But who was going to be *her* assistant?

Just then Lorraine walked in.

"You've got a new job," I said.

"Working for you?"

"For Myra."

"Yum," she said.

"That's all? No questions?"

"Did you find a replacement for me?"

"Yes," I said, suddenly remembering Lolita shouting after me: *Do you know where I can get a job?*

FIVE

You are in Rome, the day Lorraine decided that everything in the world was round. The sun struck the gilt cupolas of early morning Rome, our hotel window seemed to look out in all directions at once, the people hurrying by in cars, bicycles and on foot looked fat, round and content. So Lorraine had something there. Rome was round, the Colosseum was round, and the feeling of life in general had a lazy, rounded-out quality. Lorraine had this to say as well:

"I had a dream, an incredibly round dream in which a plump Renaissance angel came to me and said: 'Go to Via Agostino and buy round gold bracelets for Brandon and Myra.'"

It is useless to argue with Lorraine's dreams. Myra pointed, in vain, to her jewelry box wherein six or seven gold bracelets shone delicately. I argued, also in vain, that I can't stand ornaments of any sort.

What is more, there was a jewelry store on Via Agostino. The pointy-headed guy at the glass counter is the *non-capisco* clerk; he's looking at Lorraine with the accumulated fear of his twenty years in the gold trade; he simply does not understand even though his English isn't bad (he goes to Chicago a lot, on business).

"It's simple," says Lorraine. "These, Signor Carli, are my slaves."

Myra and I exchanged a quick glance of astonishment. There had been no talk of slaves in the angel's command, but Lorraine enjoys improving her dreams.

"Your slaves, *signorina?*" Maybe his American isn't so good after all; "slaves" might mean "friends" in Texas or wherever these whacky Americanos are from.

"Yes," says the terrible beauty, I want you to measure their ankles and weld two gold bracelets around them."

This is really too much. At this point I feel like bursting out laughing. Not only is Lorraine going too far, she is going straight off her rocker.

"Weld, *signorina?*"

"Yes, with a torch or however you do it. You have to be careful though. I can't stand the smell of singed flesh."

I nudge Lorraine discreetly and shake my head no, but she pays no attention.

"Two simple bracelets?" repeats Signor Carli dreamily, thinking *it must have been that second Cinzano at lunch....*

"And I want you to engrave this on the bracelets."

Back on familiar turf, Signor Carli is visibly relieved (writing, pencil, paper, message), and he puts the point of his perfectly sharpened pencil on the custom-made paper of his leatherbound pad.

"I want you to write on one 'Myra Kaminski,' that's M, Y, etcetera…. 'Property of Lorraine, Roma,' and the date…. On the other one …"

"Property, *signorina?*"

"P, R, O, etcetera…."

"On the other one, 'Brandon Stone, Property …' that's P, R, O, etcetera … 'of Lorraine, Roma,' and the date. Got it, Jack?"

An immense smile travels around the point of Signor Carli's pointy head. He points at us and says: "Ah, slaves, *amore, amore!*"

Happy he has solved the puzzle, he pays us not another look but simply seems to flourish around Lorraine. He blooms all around her with admiration. While he calculates the suggested cost, he even offers bits of personal philosophy: "We Romans understand love. We are all slaves of love."

Both Myra and I are in a state of shock. When a young boy, summoned from the wings by Signor Carli, begins fiddling with a tape measure around my ankle, I lift my leg accommodatingly even though my original instinct is to kick him in the shins.

When it's Myra's turn, she thrusts her aristocratic leg at young Giovanni, who simply seems to have forgotten numbers as he fiddles with his blushing tape around the lady's foot. Myra lifts her leg higher for better measuring, and Giovanni's eyes go straight up her leg into the depths of her unbuttoned skirt. Even Signor Carli, who seems to see through Giovannotto's eyes, smiles and flushes without knowing why.

"Can we have these delivered and welded at the Hotel Victoria?"

"Of course, *signorina*, of course!"

"Come now," says Lorraine, overdoing the slave bit. She goes ahead of us to the glass door of the shop, opens it and holding it for a moment, she turns toward Signor Carli, whom she knows to be still staring. "*Grazie!*" Then she wiggles her index finger at him.

On the street I can't wait to give it to the young waif. I look at her sternly, but before I can open my mouth, she pouts and says sweetly: "I hope you're not mad...."

The hell I'm not.

"I don't mind the idea too much," says Myra, "but I hate the bracelet bit!"

For a moment my whole illusion of control slips away. Just who was going to build whom, where? Seemed like instead of my putting Lorraine in my story, I was being put in hers.

"What we do in the hotel ..." Myra was saying, "is one thing ... but we must maintain a bit of decorum in public...."

Could it all have started in Naples?"

In Naples, shortly after our arrival, we took a beautiful suite of rooms at the Capri Hotel, the corner suite that looks on the Mediterranean with the Capri outlined in the horizon like a sun-drenched nymph.

When we were safely installed in our room, we

opened all the windows to let the sweet, sunny breeze in.

"*Magnifico!*" exclaimed Myra.

Lorraine gave an Indian shout, lifted her arms above her head and got rid of her clothes in three determined movements. "Ah," she said, leaning over the little balcony protruding like a marble tooth over the blue sea.

She cupped her breasts and offered them as some kind of ritual to the Mediterranean. This private ritual was witnessed by at least one fisherman floating on the Bay of Naples with his binoculars pointing at the famous room in the Capri Hotel.

Myra soon followed suit, and she too went naked onto the balcony and put her arm around Lorraine's shoulders. The view of their two graceful backs, buttocks and legs is my coat of arms. This view is engraved on my mind like a rose on a tombstone, with the Mediterranean engulfing it from all sides. They stood there like that for a considerable time, until finally I tore off my clothes and joined them.

Then we ordered champagne. When it came, Lorraine was wearing Myra's chemise, which barely concealed her butt, Myra was wearing her Indian blanket and I had my trousers on. So everything looked normal when the waiters wheeled the champagne into the room. I tipped them generously.

We started making love. That is, Lorraine commanded me to make love to Myra first. It was usually Myra who asked me to make love to Lorraine first.

"This is not our custom," Myra protested. "I'm not sure I'll like it."

It was a curious sensation, the same sensation as she

*must have gotten when I ordered Brandon to fuck her. I
don't know if I like the reverse. Actually, I do. I felt, as I
lay under Brandon, that if I did not give my best I would
receive the sting of a lash across my butt. Once when I
lifted my eyes toward Lorraine, I saw that she was perfectly capable of it. She stood over us, watching us severely.*

Next day we went to Pompeii. If you've been there,
forgive me. If you haven't, you must go. The place
was created by the historical imagination of a volcano. It was this volcano, staring at the busy city of
Pompeii in a perfect autumn light one day, that
decided to keep that particular image of the city forever. To this purpose, it began to gush gobs of lava
across the city and encase everything in casts. The
whole city froze like that, in full swing. This volcano
is my favorite argument for fiction.

The city of Pompeii, thus frozen, is full of guided
tours and such, but with a little cunning you can get
to wander by yourself and collect impressions. And
once you're in, you begin feeling a great current of
sympathy with those Romans, many of whom were
caught in poses of extreme pleasure.

From Myra's diary:

*As much as I've heard said and as much as I've seen (in
books) of this place, I cannot say it has prepared me. Being
here, in the heart of a bacchanalia, inspires you to see the
possibilities of love. Not only is everything sanctioned,
but there are hints in the poses of the people that there is
so much more—feelings for which there are no pictures,
games for which there are no names. The imagination of
human bodies for pleasure is practically endless, in spite
of what the sex manuals say.*

To Lorraine it was a dream come true. If until now she had still been a little intimidated by our authority, she now saw youth worshiped for the same reason we worshiped her. She became fully conscious of her power, her beauty and her ability to command through it. This is the point where the tender benefactor of kids turned into the full-blooded lioness who knew her rights.

In Rome we partied almost too much. It was a full three days and nights filled with intoxication (champagne, sex, nightclubs, etcetera), but then we finally did get to work.

I gave Lorraine a couple of hundred dollars to use for play while Myra and I started calling on a number of people we had to see.

The old Belgian antiquarian, Monsieur Rayez, was renowned the world over for his mysterious collection of erotica, including Greek vases, Persian miniatures and Renaissance chalices. The world also know Monsieur Rayez as one of the most inaccessible men anywhere. It took a long letter, five telephone calls and a vast exchange of references before we were summoned to the sanctuary.

Monsieur Rayez occupied a whole building in the old ghetto in Trastevere, an ancient part of Rome neatly separated from the rest by the Tiber.

The grizzled little man did not bother to greet us. A maid opened the door and entrusted us to the care of a young man, secretary to Monsieur Rayez, who smiled curtly and invited us to view the collection.

"There is much, you understand, that can't be shown," he said. "Monsieur does not trust anybody. Your good name, Dr. Kaminski, has opened these doors, but I urge you, please, no photographs. You can use your notebook to sketch."

We had not stated the real purpose of our visit. We had explained our interest academically. If anyone had known that we were searching for a particular object we would not have been allowed in. All the collections we viewed were protected precisely against seekers for a particular object. Even though Professor Kaminski's theory stood behind us to lend scientific legitimacy, who was to separate us from all the fanatics who, throughout the ages, had searched for a sacred cup or chalice which would give them eternal youth and everlasting life? These fanatics, known to every art collector in the world, would generally stop at nothing to obtain the object they desired.

The walls of the paneled and mirrored rooms we went through were covered with paintings. Not necessarily erotic, mostly Dutch masters and minor Renaissance painters. But suddenly we were in a room unlike the others. It was a stern room, white walls. Lying delicately on velvet stands, there was a series of Greek reliefs which Myra identified instantly as having once surrounded the sacred pit of Persephone, queen of the underworld. The main panel showed a goddess arising from the earth, with two attendants holding a veil to conceal her. Her two attendants were crouching, holding the veil just above her navel. On the sides were a nude flute-girl and a heavily veiled woman burning incense. The flute-girl was in a sensual trance, while the veiled woman was thoughtful. And so they went, twelve pieces in all, from the winged boy holding the scales to Pirithous' bride being firmly grasped by the centaur. But Myra noticed that one piece was missing, since the myth, which she was familiar with was not concluded in the reliefs.

She made rapid-fire sketches of the reliefs, puzzled by the missing piece. I couldn't but think of the incredibly urgent nature of this art. It wasn't *ancient* art in any sense, it spoke to our situation here and now. I began seeing the three of us superimposed over the marbled images in the room. We fit the role of those gods and goddesses just fine.

We skipped through the Persian miniatures because, as it often happens when concentrating on Greek art, it takes a whole readjustment of perspective to see anything else. Greek art is so perfect, it carries such authority, it is hard to shake its charm.

Monsieur Rayez himself gave us a three-minute audience before we left. He was so tiny and wrinkled, I saw a gnome. He said: "I try not to be terribly moralistic concerning people's reasons for seeing my collection. But I am curious...."

"A strictly scientific inquiry," said Myra.

The old man gave a dry laugh. "There are overt reasons, of course. Far from me to deny their importance. But what is the purpose of your study?"

As if not hearing him, Myra asked abruptly: "There should be thirteen reliefs of Persephone. Do you possess the last one?"

Monsieur Rayez studied her quietly for a few moments. "The conclusion of the myth is not on a relief. Only twelve reliefs surrounded the pit. If there is a thirteenth, it is not a relief but rather a sacramental object in the hand of the goddess. No one has ever described it. It seems that it was stolen early in the fifth century by barbarians." Turning to me, the old man said, "And you?"

"Brandon Stone, sir. I am a writer. I am Dr. Kaminski's companion."

"Ah!" he said.

"What did it look like?" insisted Myra.

"No one has seen it. And now, if you will forgive me, I must have my injection."

I couldn't help thinking later, when Myra and I sipped a meditative espresso at a little *baretto*, that the old man had seen through us, had seen through us so far, in fact, he had glimpsed Lorraine shopping in Rome and conducting, at that very moment, a flirtatious conversation with a good-looking Italian man.

"You are so happy, *signorina*," said the man. "Would you like to have a drink?"

"Sure," said Lorraine, imagining (rightly) that the man would carry her bags for her. (She bought six pairs of black silk underwear at a lingerie shop, a zippered motorcycle jacket, a hat with a short veil and one pair of black riding boots.)

"Are you married?" she asked, looking at him through her Pernod.

The man unwrapped his brown shades from around his face and smiled. "*I am, signorina*, I most certainly am. But it is a very unhappy marriage!"

"Too many bambinos?"

"Only five," he said modestly.

Lorraine whistled admiringly.

"Are you?" the man said.

"Am I what?"

"Married."

"Oh yes," said Lorraine. "I have a husband and a wife."

"Two?" he said.

"Yes." Lorraine lowered her voice. "But they are hardly enough for me. I have to go out and...."

"No ..." the man said compassionately, feeling the heat rise, certain, almost certain this time, that he had fallen prey to that much-imagined sex maniac (female).

"Yes." Lorraine shook her head sadly.

"I know a little *pensione* just around the corner, if you like...."

"Oh no, no ... I have to go back to my husband and wife and ask them for some more money before the stores close...."

The man looked up sharply. He was thunderstruck. Could this clean little American *ragazza* be asking him for money? Could she be a tart? Impossible.

"I can led you a little money," he said. "We'll go shopping now, and I'll buy you what you want, a gift from me...."

"Let's go," Lorraine said.

Lorraine had no idea what she wanted to buy so she went from store to store on the Via Veneto, unable to make up her mind. Finally, she found a silver crucifix with a silver chain and she decided to buy it. Her companion was terrified, to tell the truth. He was terrified of the cost, which he knew would be a lot, and also because of the symbol. But when Lorraine slipped the cross around her long neck with her hands raised girlishly just so, he felt a second wave of affection.

"My name is Alonso," he said. "My mother is Spanish."

He bought her the necklace and carried her packages. Lorraine walked a bit behind him, whistling a bird tune.

A true Roman, she thought. A great nose, a beautiful sinewy body. I wish I had him for a slave too. Her imagination, which never failed her, conjured up a vast slave population, all young, all handsome, over which she ruled whimsically, cruelly, furiously. A tingle ran from head to foot.

Alonso paid the *padrone* for the room and, without speaking, they slipped upstairs. There was one bed, a dresser with a mirror and a bassinet.

This is it, thought Lorraine excitedly. She took everything off with the exception of the silver crucifix, which she felt dig into her flesh when Alonso took her standing up.

Lorraine wasn't back when Myra and I got to the hotel. We ordered dinner to be brought upstairs and sat at the window looking at the neon signs lighting up Rome. We ate silently.

"Is it possible," mused Myra in a letter to her husband, *"that the missing relief is the chalice we are searching for? A chalice that synthesizes perhaps not only the myth of Persephone but the entire experience of Greek eroticism. If it is indeed a chalice and it exists, it must have been invaluable to the later Renaissance piece which you postulate. But it could be the main object...."*

Lorraine still hadn't returned, so we decided to go to a movie. After the movie we'd come back for Lorraine, maybe go to a nightclub.

I dressed in evening clothes, and Myra put on a beautiful dress with an ermine stole. We looked dashing and aristocratic, a luxury which Lorraine in her youthful disdain rarely allowed us.

On the street we walked arm to arm (no taxi, we were in the center of Roma), and we could feel envious looks. Italians love luxury, dressy clothes, elegance, aristocracy. I love it too. Walking like this alone with Myra, I felt for the first time since our arrival how enormously tired I was, how hard it was to keep hard (excuse me) day and night, how hard (and yet how delightful) to be at the whim of that little sex tyrant. But this too was enjoyable.

The men and women on the street were incredibly good looking. Myra squeezed my arm whenever she saw something gorgeous, and since she did it disregarding gender, my arm was rapidly turning black and blue.

We saw some movie or other (I think it was a de Sica picture) and took pleasure in sitting there in the dark, with our arms dangling lightly in each other's laps.

In her diary Myra said:

How easy it is without Lorraine! How easy and how tame, somehow. It reminds me of a poem by Lewis MacAdams: I look/ on more sex/ as a threat. And even as I write the word "threat," I know I love Lorraine's threat, her fierce looks, her strong thighs, her impertinent breasts with her nipples pointing up, her greed, her power....

If I were called upon to explain that poem, I would also see it as the description of a very happy state in which sex has suffused the body, turning it into a red-hot erotic vase, thus de-emphasizing the genitals as the primary source of pleasure.

We were charged, both of us. Even as we sat there, in the darkness of a foreign-language movie, we could draw the energy of the room toward us. We were involuntarily magnetized. Powerful.

Lorraine was furious when we walked in softly, arm in arm.

"Where did you go without me?" she screamed.

"Not far, precious," said Myra.

"We went to a movie."

"And left me all alone, dammit!" She was sulking. "I should leave you is what I should do!"

That was a threat. Recognized.

"Look," said Myra, "would you like to hit me?"

"Yesss."

"Where?"

"Bare your butt," she said and started unwrapping the package where her black riding boots were. She tore the package open and pulled on her boots. She did it all so gymnastically, so convinced of what she was doing, I had a hard time keeping a straight face.

"And what are you giggling at?" she screamed at me.

"I don't want to be left out," I said.

"You take off all your clothes and lie face up!" she ordered me.

I complied, as did Myra. I had a view of the ceiling and of Myra on all fours with a bare ass, as well as of Lorraine fully dressed with her black boots on, standing there like a determined Nazi V. All she lacked was a whip, but she didn't need one. With a firm blow to the crotch she landed Myra on the other side of the room. Without waiting to see the impact, she turned to me as if to kick me fully in the balls but then stopped, the tip of her boot only an inch away from my outraged masculinity. In my everlasting puzzlement I became erect. Lorraine slowly caressed my erection with the tip of her boot. Suddenly, Myra stood up and gave the child a terrible whack across the face. Lorraine faced her, and the two of them fell to the floor fighting.

The confusion generated by this incident was loud. There was a knock at the door from the hotel establishment. They wanted to know what the racket was all about. I explained without opening the door and with a certain tremor in my voice that nothing was the matter, we were merely practicing karate if they wanted to come in and see. Fortunately, they were satisfied, because the girls hadn't stopped fighting for one second.

Trembling, Lorraine apologized: "I don't know what came over me. I've been having these slave fantasies...."

Three days passed and, eventually, Myra forgave her. I hadn't been particularly outraged, merely amused. Our life together took, once again, the sweet quality of its beginnings. We didn't refer to the incident at all. I had almost forgotten the whole thing until Lorraine had her dream about the angel and, subsequently, ordered us slave bracelets.

And today there was another knock at the door. I prepared to answer arrogantly, so I opened the door as wide as possible; but instead of the valet, Giovannotto stood there, accompanied by a musta-chioed man built like a horseshoer. He had a box of tools in one hand.

"It is your order, *signor!*" he said to me.

"Ah," exclaimed Lorraine, "drive right in!"

Ceremoniously, Giovannotto unwrapped two thick gold bracelets contained in a leather box. The horseshoer followed suit, opening the toolbox to extract a delicate welding torch.

What could we do? The thought occurred to me that Myra won't stand for it and, surely, she rose from the chair where she had been reading and turned a fierce gaze in the men's direction.

"Please," Lorraine said softly, "I will never ask anything else of you!"

Why Myra acceded I will never know. I don't, for that matter, know why I did either. Enough to say, flames of blue gas left the welding torch to affix two gold rings to our ankles.

When the men left we didn't speak for a long time. I certainly wasn't the one to break the silence. Lorraine was the first one to speak. She said meekly: "You are mine now, I love you."

"Hmmm," I said, trying to feel light about the whole thing, put it in its proper perspective.

And then, as if driven by the same thought, we pulled our feet up to look at the bracelets there and after reading what they said, we burst out laughing: The bracelet eternally welded to my foot said: MYRA KAMINSKI. PROPERTY OF LORRAINE, ROMA, MAY 1975. And Myra's bracelet said, no doubt, BRANDON STONE, etcetera.

Lorraine joined us laughing but drew her breath in long enough to say: "Now you are Myra and she is Brandon!"

"And you are a little bitch," said Myra, picking up the book she had been reading and thinking *I can't believe it. I must concentrate on finding the chalice, lest I go crazy.*

SIX

You probably don't want to hear a lecture on zippers and family affairs, but I have no choice. A number of zippers and a number of Lorraine's family affairs came together during the rest of our stay in Italy as in a kind of Dali painting.

To begin with, we had between us six thousand dollars. This was the rest of the ten thousand dollars from the generous History Department of the University of Michigan. The remaining forty thousand dollars was to be given annually, ten thousand per annum during the next four years. My Aunt Dorothy's money was still tangled up in legal goo. Six thousand dollars, you will say, is a lot of money. Yes, if you are taking a two-week trip to Italy and, yes, if you are alone and don't have to spend any of it on *zippers*. But Lorraine liked to buy zippered things. She'd gone bananas over leather jackets with thousands of zippers and leather pants with zippers. There was a possibility that she might run out of sartorial items and begin buying crocodiles by way of extending her passion metaphorically. And there were six more countries on our visiting list. So, naturally, I was worried about money. Short of wiring Myra's husband, we had to be careful and, naturally, we could not economize on champagne (breakfast, lunch and dinner) or move into cheaper hotels because this would have put a cramp in our style.

One morning mail came. Lorraine's father wrote to his daughter (for the family) a letter that amounted to excommunication.

"You promised," this missive said, *"to join a sorority and see to your studies. Somehow, we, your mother, your brother, your sisters and I, do not believe that you are in Europe for serious business. The picture you sent us (in which you look healthy, thank God) gives the impression rather that you are having a ball. There is time to have a ball, and there is time to study. You must return to school immediately. I pay good money for it. I don't want to see it wasted, especially with the present situation of the economy....*

"Would you like me to write to your father?" said Myra solicitously. "I am, after all, a professor, and you are working for the school."

Lorraine burst into tears. "This awful thing had to come now. Pop's really upset."

For the rest of the day Lorraine wrote a long letter to her parents, and Myra and I helped her with her spelling. It was a depressing day.

In the evening, however, we went to a discotheque and danced until morning. We slept until two in the afternoon next day, and by the time we got up it was too late to mail the letter and, besides, Lorraine was feeling better. So she zipped the laborious answer to Pop's concern in one of her many pockets and promptly forgot about it.

That afternoon, the word came from the Vatican Chancery that we had received permission to delve into the stacks of the fabulous Vatican Library. After our visit to Monsieur Rayez, Myra had decided that the next step ought to be researching little-known medieval literature to see if the subject we were searching for was in any measure alluded to.

A grumpy and suspicious priest myopically accepted us. The gilded little room through which the mellow sun poured its benediction on our slight hangovers was a niche of peace and scholarly calm. We made notes of books and manuscripts we wanted to see (the far-from-complete indexes were ceiling high). Around 4 P.M. we rang a little bell, and a stern-looking Jesuit father appeared to assist us through the library labyrinths.

I must confess to a certain awe as we descended into these tremendous receptacles of information, these fabulous records of human history. Our tiny bodies slid along the trail of Father Benedetti's robes like snails toward the secret heart of the cabbage. My heart beat faster as we went past the still secret archives of the popes, past the forbidden books of the alchemists (which the Church collected), past the infamous Index Malleficorum in which Copernicus was still buried, past all that was past and still unknown. The section we were about to visit was only partially forbidden, and we were going to see things which only a few privileged scholars had seen. We were going to look at illuminated manuscripts of the fifteenth century, manuscripts concerned with the love heresies of the Bogumilians and other sects which had run afoul of the Church by claiming to go back to the original word of Christ. That word was love.

Father Benedetti, in spite of his severely lined Jesuitic face, was a discreet man. He left us alone with a mound of books and excused himself. He would pick us up in a couple of hours, he said. He wished us happy dreaming with a whimsical smile which made me like him instantly. I have had occasion to notice how much more human certain priests are than men who claim to know the world by having thrashed about in it.

Suddenly, we were surrounded by thousands of chalices, cups and grails. The pages of the ancient parchments were weighted down with references of every kind about holy vessels with magical powers which had eluded detection.

A gold-leafed chalice representing the Vision of Ezekiel was said to have disappeared during the sacking of Rome by the Goths. As far as the author knew, this gold cup showed a winged creature of perverse charm and immense knowledge leading the holy man through the seven circles of heaven, where the holy dwelt in sensual bliss. Another extremely magical cup of Syriac origin was said to cure ills. And then we found something extraordinary: an almost-faded drawing of a Greek chalice. The barely visible figures were immediately recognizable as similar in nature to the Persephone reliefs. This cup, the scribe claimed, was seen three times during the Christian era at the tables of three differ-

ent popes, only to disappear with the French con-
quest in the fifteenth century.

Myra and I experienced such sensual pleasure at
the sight of this faded object that a nearby Wedding
of Cana in the open pages of another book spread its
luminous leafage through us and embraced us with
its roots. All my life I have gotten an erotic sensation
from old libraries and museums. I had never found
anyone to share my excitement until now. It was as if
Myra and I had been joined in this ancient obsession.
Myra's left hand rested dreamily on the page of the
old book.

I don't know what might have happened if Father
Benedetti's kind face hadn't reminded us of the time.
Glancing at the picture, the father said: "Yes, that
story has often intrigued me."

"Do you know where this chalice might be?"

"I'm afraid not. The French Church has made several inquiries. There seems to be a prevailing opinion
that the cup is in France. Beyond that, no one knows.
But it is late. The staff is leaving the library."

We had dinner at a little Trastevere restaurant. We
were wonderfully exhausted. Could this whole fantastic project really have originated in the History
Department of the University of Michigan and Dr.
Kaminski's brain? I must from now on give a lot more
credit to the obscure reasons that bloom in the minds
of our academics. This chalice we were searching for
had never fascinated me until now. I must admit that,
from the beginning, I felt a bit skeptical about the
entire practical side of this venture. But I was beginning to catch the fever.

At the hotel there was another letter (special
delivery) to Lorraine, from her father.

Dear Daughter:
   You must return. It you stay, you risk our affection as well as our financial support.

"I will risk it," said Lorraine. She tore up the letter she'd written earlier and wrote a much terser message, without apologies. She put this in one of her many pockets, drew the zipper and resolved to send it the next day.

It was nine o'clock, and I hope that you never have to watch any Italian television. Nevertheless, this is exactly what we were doing.

The telephone rang.

"There is a man at the desk," the clerk said, "who would like to speak to Signorina Lorraine."

"That must be Alonso," said Lorraine.

We looked at her, surprised. We didn't know about any Alonso. The little slave owner had a colonial policy. Myra and I smiled at each other.

"Why don't you ask him up?" I said.

"Tell him to come right up."

Alonso Silvestri was dressed with extreme care and elegance.

"This is my family," said Lorraine. "I told you about them."

Alonso was a fantastically pleasant and witty man. With that friendly and unselfconscious braggadocio of a man of the world, he charmed us instantly.

He was a lawyer working for a government study group on the preservation of artworks in Italy, a study, he told us, that had been going on for ten years and, knowing the Italian government, could go on for ten more. A great number of places closed to tourists and the general public came under his commission's jurisdiction.

"Signor Silvestri," said Myra, "we are fortunate to run into you."

"Call me Alonso. It is your young friend here who is really to blame."

Lorraine, at the height of her youthful pride, surveyed all of us with magnanimity.

"What do you say," Alonso said, "to going out to a little place I know? It is a place I am sure no non-Roman knows about. It is a club really."

Delighted.

If we had been in England, this place would have been a gentlemen's club. We spilled out of Alonso's Porsche into the arms of an amiable doorman who took our jackets and Lorraine's leather one as if they were mink coats.

Inside, the place was plastered with photographs of famous movie stars, directors—a picture gallery of Italy's important people.

Casually, Alonso approached a table where several younger men sat with their extremely elegant and refined ladies.

"Alonso!" A prematurely gray young man stood and motioned him to sit down. "Who are your friends?"

Introductions properly followed, and soon we were sitting in extremely pleasant and merry company.

Paolo Lars was a film producer, a friend of Silvestri's. He was outraged about a recent bombing at Cinecittà, the Italian film studio.

"Can you imagine?" he said. "Anyone wanting to bomb Cinecittà! I am a Marxist myself, and I think most of the studio people are. A technician was injured! A technician, *sangre di Dio*, a man with a six-year membership in the party!"

"These are Maoists, Paolo!" said Maria Leone, whom I then recognized as the star of the film Myra and I had seen the other night. "They are savage beasts, these Maoists. I don't understand them at all."

Giovanni Creghi was a journalist for *Il Corriere Della Sera*. He said: "I understand them perfectly. Any Marxist success in Italy is the end of them. They are saboteurs."

"Maybe not," a stark young man said.

"Carlo! *Per la madonna!*" exclaimed Paolo. "You are not one of them, I hope!"

The young man said nothing. "A snake in Eden!" said the outraged Signor Lars. "Can't you see what these terrorist bombs are doing? They are preparing us for a new dark age!"

"Carlo, Paolo, *per favore,*" intervened Maria. To us: "Whenever Italian men begin quarreling about politics, there is no end to it!"

Everyone laughed. Turning to me, Paolo asked: "What brings you to Italy?"

"We are doing research for an American university...." I said.

Alonso said quickly: "*Erotica* research!"

"Ah," Paolo said with a fake sigh of relief. "I imagined some extremely dull research for a minute."

"And your lovely companions?" asked Maria, whose eyes had already lit on Lorraine's youthful charms.

"Dr. Kaminski," I said, "is the true scientist among us. Lorraine is our assistant."

"Very interesting," Maria said.

"This might be an impertinent question to this

company," said Giovanni Creghi, "but how is your research funded?"

"Always the journalist," said Maria.

"On a university grant...."

"Those crazy American universities...." Paolo Lars was amused. "It would make a good film: *American Archaeologist Finds Sex!*"

"All in good order, Lars!" said Creghi. "You always steal my best ideas! A university grant could not be very much...."

"Sufficient," said Myra.

"I sense a story," Creghi went on doggedly. "Perhaps you could write a popularized account of you journey for *Il Corriere*...."

"I'm afraid our combined Italian isn't worth a red herring," I hastened to add.

"That is no problem," said Creghi. "I will take care of that. We could use pseudonyms if you don't care to get in trouble back home."

"Italians are forever crazy about the whims of rich *Americanos*," said Paolo.

"Rich we are not!" Lorraine put in.

"Why then," shouted Creghi, who had all of it already figured out, "I come and see you with my tape recorder and you will receive a handsome sum from my paper. Let's say, five hundred thousand lire...."

A rapid calculation: One dollar is six hundred lire. Around four thousand dollars. My heart began to beat fast.

Creghi raved on: "Three American scientists, two beautiful women and a young man, are digging through the world's erotic art to study their reactions as well as the art.... Why, they will go crazy.... Where else are you going?"

"To France, to Eastern Europe perhaps," announced Myra.

"To Communist Europe?" said Creghi. "That's fabulous!"

"Not so fast," Paolo cut in. "I want the movie rights!"

I was beginning to swim in visions. Money. It's a funny thing. All my life I needed it. The minute I stopped thinking about *earning* it, it came to me of its own accord. And I hadn't even gotten Aunt Dorothy's money, which had started it all. Thank you, dear aunt!

Unexpectedly, Myra said: "I am not sure our research lends itself to popularization."

Everyone laughed. "Even God, my dear," said Creghi, "lends himself to popularization. It is you Americans who have discovered that wonderful secret."

"And besides," Lorraine said, "I would love to be in the movies!"

"Oh no," I said, "that part will have to be played by someone else. You have to stay with us. Lead the flock, you know...."

It is so easy to lose this flirtatious kid.

"I will do the part," said Maria Leone, "but first, my dear, I must get to know you."

"This is incredible!" exclaimed Signor Lars. "I can't believe it! You are Italy's hottest new star! This will be a winner! Let's talk figures. The rights to your journey. How much?"

I'm not very comfortable in lire. My head began to spin.

"You better be careful," said Alonso. "Good thing I'm here to offer legal counsel. Paolo is a very rich man."

"Get him for all he's worth!" said Maria.

"My good friends ..." Paolo gestured derisively. "I offer you one hundred fifty thousand dollars, and that is *dollars*," he underlined.

"Dollars?" I repeated after him.

The table fell quiet. Even in the world of the super-rich, big deals command attention.

"Two-hundred and twenty-five thousand ..." said Lorraine. "And for that I'll throw in my family's story too. I am pure WASP—you know, a real American girl."

"*Dio!*" Maria said. "A real American girl ... I want one."

"One hundred fifty thousand *dollars*," said Paolo.

I looked at Myra. She was studying me with extreme interest. It was the only time I felt the weight of her Ph.D. She looked at me like a teacher at a student taking a test.

"Myra," I said slyly, "why don't you do the talking?"

"I'm merely a poor slave," she answered.

"So am I," I said, mockingly throwing my hands in the air.

"So that's that." Lorraine smiled, only too happy to take over. "Well then, I say we take it."

We solemnly shook hands and ordered champagne.

"This whole bill is on us," I said.

Outside, as everybody got into their cars, Maria took Lorraine by her shoulders and whispered something in her ear.

"Sure," Lorraine said, "I would love to."

But Alonso stood there. "I'm so sorry, Maria," he said, "but this child has to go to bed; she has a hard day tomorrow. And besides, I brought her here."

Maria dipped into her purse and wrote something down on a piece of paper. She gave this to Lorraine. "*Ciao, cara,*" she said and kissed the child hard on the lips.

At the hotel Alonso, who had brought us back, asked our permission to tarry a bit with Lorraine.

We gave him that and went upstairs.

They tarried for exactly an hour and fifty-five minutes.

We slept like the rich babies we were, twined into each other.

The morning began with another letter from Pop (special delivery express insured).

If you do not call or answer by midnight, you're out of my will, daughter!

Lorraine tore up last night's terse message, which she had forgotten to mail again. She started to cry.

"I can't believe they will ignore you when they find out what you're worth," said Myra.

"It's not that," sobbed Lorraine. "It's just that … I love Pop. I promised him I'd join a sorority…."

"Pop," said Myra judiciously, "wanted you to join a sorority in order to stay a virgin. You're not that, you know."

"But I am, I really am," cried Lorraine.

After laughing for a few minutes we proceeded to undress the child and examine her with thorough care.

"No," Myra concluded after she had examined her with nimble fingers, "nope."

I confirmed this too, in my own male chauvinist way.

This crisis having passed, we prevailed on her to write a simple letter to Pop, explaining innocently what she was doing.

She did, and the zippered pocket of her leather jacket absorbed this one too. The jacket was, I might add, on the floor with the rest of her leather paraphernalia, lying in a heap like the gear of a skinny-dipping Hell's Angel. Lorraine liked to write in the nude with the pencil squeezed between her teeth, on her belly, with her ankles raised and crossed in the air.

The room telephone rang at this moment. It was Signor Creghi with his tape recorder. He came up to our room, dressed in a white sports suit with wraparound blue shades.

We made ourselves comfortable and began telling Creghi, who was not awkward in the slightest, the story of our adventure, beginning with my Aunt Dorothy. The three of us had agreed beforehand not to mention the chalice we were looking for, thus making our trip a sort of general search rather than a secret mission. This was best, we felt, to protect ourselves in case we were found out.

"This is fabulous," the journalist kept exclaiming, "just fabulous! Unfortunately, it is only the beginning of your story. You must send me the sequels! Otherwise you'll never get the second half of your money," he said, pulling from his coat, at that moment, a bank draft for two hundred fifty thousand lire, cashable at the Banco di Spirito Santo.

SEVEN

Myra's diary:

Can certain things go too far? How far is far? I was deter-mined (still am!) to follow everything through, but I have to assert myself! The child (I'm already calling her that, I have daughters almost her age!) is getting just a teeny bit on my nerves with the master bit. Brandon seems to take it all very equanimitously, but I thing it irks him a little. He hasn't written a single line of his Great Story.

It was raining, Myra was taking a long bath and writ-ing in her diary, Lorraine was looking at pictures in a giant illustrated book on witchcraft curled up in an armchair and I was trying to read the liner notes on an English Wagner record. But I couldn't concentrate. The scene was quiet, peaceful, domestic and lovely.

The rain outside made the turmoil of the past few weeks seem remote. Would I ever write my Great Story? Would we ever find the chalice? Would we stay friends? Questions which, like the rain, fell evenly on my mind. What if Lorraine's repentance hadn't happened? Then what? Perhaps we would still be together like this, on a rainy day, spinning through the world like a love top out of control. "Her youth just couldn't stand the strain of our wisdom," Myra said later.

Anyway, the tranquillity of that scene was a very small island in the storm of our last week in Rome.

We had, without realizing it, set in motion a vast machinery which contained implicitly the persons of Paolo Lars and Giovanni Creghi. These men were corporations, and as a result we had to sign papers, have luncheons, meet a lot of people. It distracted Myra and me. The whole laborious work of the world hit us suddenly. I was impatient to leave. We kept the telephone off the hook at least five hours a day, but it didn't stop the intrusions. We were suddenly chic, and people wanted to know us. Myra said, regretfully: "I think I've crossed the line between scholarship and life."

"Let's elope," I said.

Lorraine thought differently: "You're both old fogeys." She was having a ball. Her personal notoriety soared when a gossip columnist reported a rumor, which was only too true, of a romance between the famous Maria Leone and the Real American Girl.

The afternoon of the day we recorded our saga, Maria Leone's abnormally long limousine pulled up in front of the hotel. Lorraine got in the back with the actress, whose long fur collar covered her face, and they sped off.

I can't be sure of what happened, since Lorraine's descriptions of her extracurricular activities had become very sketchy. All I could get out of her was a description of Maria Leone's house, which should have been in Beverly Hills because it didn't sound very Italian: tall mirrors and soft rugs, room-sized bathtubs, a valid interpretation of Hollywood. Enough to say that our naughty mistress was returned to us, seemingly unharmed (though a bit preoccupied). But that wasn't nearly the end of that eventful day after we'd struck it rich.

At ten in the evening, Paolo called to tell us that his studios would make a deal whereby Creghi's tapes were not part of the rights to our story. I understood this was a kickback scheme to Creghi, who would then be selling the tapes personally as an addition. We were also to begin keeping a collective diary of our journey which could, eventually, become a book. Paolo was ready to sell international rights to the book for an agent's fee. How neatly it all takes place, I thought. Nobody loses in the end. But I didn't feel like keeping a diary, and Myra was already keeping one of her own. As for Lorraine, if her verbal gifts had had written equivalents she'd have already been rich. So I protested. "This story will be relayed orally," I said. "If you can make a book out of it we'll be glad to negotiate publication." We agreed on some rather strict pseudonyms. Lorraine became Cherry, Myra became Lenore and I was Jack Scott.

"We will pay you a first installment of thirty thousand dollars in perfect good faith. We will sign the papers tomorrow."

We rejoiced for a while, my two loves and I, in the best way which we know how, by screwing.

We were sleeping, I believe (at least I was), when suddenly I felt somebody's presence in the room, possibly moving softly through the dark. To be certain, I lay there for a few seconds listening to the noise. I nudged Myra. She was awake, but I knew Lorraine was sleeping because I could hear her regular breath. I jumped up abruptly, reaching for the light on the end table. I didn't reach it. A calm, strong voice with a heavy Roman accent said:

"For your own good, I advise you to stand still."

Lorraine woke, and she was going to scream. I knew this too somehow, and I put my hand over her mouth.

A flashlight came on, directed straight at my eyes. I couldn't see anything.

"We want the check," the man said, moving the light out of my eyes to scan random objects.

When he took the light away, I recognized Carlo, the stern, dark man at our table the other night.

"Carlo!" I said.

"It won't do you any good to recognize me," he said. "I am a soldier of Cell Number Six of the Youth Freedom Army."

"You dirty Maoist," said Myra.

"You pig!" screamed Lorraine. "That's our money!"

I put my hand on her mouth. Carlo was nervous. This is when I noticed that he was holding a giant pistol with a silencer on the end of it.

"The check is in the desk drawer."

He walked backward to the desk and pulled it

open, keeping his gun on us. He looked at the check closely.

"Where is the money from Paolo Lars?"

"We have no deal with Paolo Lars," said Myra, cool as a cucumber.

"You better not be lying. I will be back. If not me, then my comrades. This money will arm the people. Don't bother reporting this to the police. I cannot be found."

I must admit that in spite of the gun and the stern voice I had a slight feeling of unreality, as if watching a movie. Well, easy come, easy go, I thought. It was just a piece of paper. But we were really going to need Paolo's money now. When the door had shut softly after the burglar, I picked up my jacket from the floor to see if we still had our cash and my suspicion was confirmed. Our cash was also gone.

"Call the bank," said Myra. "He won't be able to cash the check. It was a bank draft. Good as gold."

Lorraine picked up the telephone and started screaming at the desk operator before I could stop her: "We've been robbed! We've been robbed!"

I pushed the receiver down. I needed time to think.

"I wouldn't involve the police," said Myra. "We are here on an American research grant. They will make political capital out of it."

"But we've been robbed!" screamed Lorraine, who could scream just like the young ingenue the gorilla held over the Empire State Building.

"Stop shouting, Lorraine, for Chrissakes!" I shouted. "You'll get your goddamn zippered lollipops. Just quit!"

"Wonderful," Myra piped in. "We are having our third three-way fight."

The hotel detective at the door wanted to know what all the ruckus was about.

"It's just a bad dream our daughter had, *signor*," I said, without deigning to open up. "I'm sorry for the trouble."

"There are other people here, you know," he grumbled.

"So sorry, really," said Myra with that crystal cool voice of hers which was to prove so effective in Communist Europe.

We didn't sleep much for the rest of the night. Lorraine got up to check the door lock every five minutes. "This wouldn't happen in Dubuque," she said.

I couldn't help laughing. "This isn't Dubuque," I said, "and you're a big girl now. You've made the gossip columns...."

In the morning we called Creghi at the offices of *Il Corriere* and told him what had happened.

He was genuinely upset. "This is Italy for you," he said. "Everywhere else in the world a man's political opinions would safely separate him from the rest! Here everything is so jumbled up no one knows what a Marxist is anymore!"

"Do you know Carlo?" I said.

"Goodness, no. He was somebody our dear Maria Leone picked up that night. She collects people like postcards."

We called Maria. She was or pretended to be shocked. "I feel terrible," she said. "I will reimburse you from my own money. That no-good *papparazzo!*" We assured her it wasn't necessary. Then she asked to talk to Lorraine, who described the frightening scene about sixty times to the sympathetic ear.

Alonso was a bit more philosophical. "You should have told Carlo that you will speak to his mama. That's one threat no Italian boy will ever ignore. The politics of our country is, unfortunately, so obscure we cannot expect you foreigners to understand it. In the same government office I work in there are seven shades of Marxists, Marxist-Catholics, Marxist-Stalinists, Marxist-Democrats, Marxist-Atheists...."

"No Maoists though?"

"Not that I know of."

This lesson in Italian realpolitik came in handy when, the next day, we got our check from Paolo and put it immediately in the hotel safe.

Our nerves a bit rattled, the three of us decided to separate for the day, each one of us going his way and meeting again in the evening.

I went immediately to the Villa Borghese and sat on the mouth of an old stone lion with my notebook. I tried to concentrate on my Great Story. The Villa Borghese is not, in case you don't know it, the Vatican. In fact, it's the exact opposite thereof. It is a park filled with pagan sculptures of satyrs and nymphs. Among these satyrs and nymphs, an elusive hooker population walks slowly by day and faster at night. I didn't know then what I know now, namely that certain sections of the park are reserved for the female persuasion while others are reserved for the male. Unbeknownst to me. I was on the male avenue. At first, I paid no attention to the seductively skinny young men with their tight pants who passed me by several times in a row. Then a more outrageous wave of subtle drag queens went by.

There wasn't anything to distinguish them from the previous young men except that instead of sailor T-shirts these boys wore makeup and undefined long-sleeved tops. But I was trying to concentrate on my Great Story. So they gathered in an ominous clump at the back of my stone lion. Slow cars cruised by, checking out the boys and me with them, it seemed.

Suddenly a car came to a stop, and someone unrolled the window. The boys began to approach, but the hand waved them away and, instead, I heard my name called:

"Brandon, Brandon!"

It was my good friend Giovanni Creghi. I walked toward the car slowly, to the pointed disgust of the boys and, safely installed, I turned to Giovanni and became speechless for what seemed like a full hour. The distinguished journalist was wearing no pants whatsoever and through his shirttails an impressive hard-on showed.

I pretended not to notice.

"What are you doing here?" I asked politely.

He shook his finger at me. "What are you doing here?"

"I was trying to think."

"Everybody knows," said Giovanni, demurely pulling part of his shirttail over the offensive erection, "that this is boys' row in the Villa Borghese."

"I'm sorry," I said.

"Don't be sorry. But are you sure ..." he asked, leaning tentatively toward me, "that you're not one of the boys?"

"Quite sure...."

"Ah," he sighed, "it's just my luck. The girls have

all the best. Would you kindly give me my trousers from the back seat?"

I leaned back and got his trousers. He stopped the car and put them on. "Now that I am respectable once more, where would you like to go for coffee?"

We went for coffee to the Piazza del Populo and pretended to each other that nothing had ever happened.

Myra, in her first blast of freedom since we had arrived, hesitated between going to the Anthropological Museum or just walking leisurely and at random through Rome. She picked the latter.

She walked, as luck would have it, to the central train station in Rome, another notorious hooker territory, and sat on the edge of the beautiful fountain there. There were some bookstalls next to the fountain, and she proposed to browse for a minute.

A tired hooker, twice Myra's age, sat next to her on the fountain and spat into the water.

"Had a hard day?" Dr. Kaminski asked sympathetically.

The older woman viewed Myra suspiciously. "You're one of these young girls who take away my living," she said in venomous Italian.

"No, no," Myra protested, "I'm an American tourist."

"Ah." She became friendly, "You can't believe what's happening. The whole world gets free pussy. My queer brother makes more than I do with men."

"Does your brother…?"

"Ah, yes, *signora*. Sometimes he goes out with the same men I do. It is terrible, it is a very hard life."

Half an hour later, the two women were comfortably seated at the kitchen table of a small apartment drinking coffee. The neighbors and the children in the courtyard below made an awful racket.

The hooker told her life story. Her life story (with all due respect to Myra's faulty Italian):

All my life I suffered from stupidity. When I was young I gave it away free, and now that I'm old I'm lucky if some-one doesn't say after they throw me a few lire: What did you do when you were young? You must have a big nest egg somewhere! It doesn't do to tell them no because nobody believes a hooker. I will tell you a secret, signora: *I am a grandmother! My little Robertita will be four in June. I hate men. My own father couldn't earn enough to keep his family fed and now, now all the young girls. Why, there are even, forgive me for saying so, young American girls like you, well-dressed, from a good family, who work the* stazione. *But why am I telling you all this? If I were smarter I could have gotten myself an American and left the country. That was after the war. When there were enough good-looking American soldiers around here I could have gotten two of them. One to keep me happy and one to keep me rich. But now it's almost over. I can see one day when I come out, my good friend Enrico, il poliziotto, will come up to me and say: You must retire now, Flora. You are an embarrassment to the other girls. And why, may I ask you? My legs are still beautiful, once I had a part in a movie....*

As Myra strained her ears to pick up all the woman's arguments with herself (*An Unfair Argument With Existence*, she thought, *thank you, Lawrence*), Lorraine was taking a huge bubble bath in a marble bathtub the size of a room.

Sitting on the edge of this pool (worthy of antiquity!) Maria Leone solicitously touched the slender creature with an enormous sponge. Maria was dressed in flowing silk veils. The discreetly hidden speakers wove Debussy's *Afternoon of a Faun* around the two nymphs. The golden light from the skylight above the pool touched off delicate sparks of color. It was a quiet and remarkable scene of which little else can be said without marring its perfection.

When the three of us met that night we were all satisfied in many ways with our souls, and the shock of the robbery had worn off.

Having found a new (temporary) slave in Maria, Lorraine wasn't at all tyrannical, and a kind of bliss reigned between us. Maria Leone smothered Lorraine in presents, and this had such a balmy effect on her soul, we had almost forgotten her little whims by the time we made ready to leave beautiful Roma.

One more fact stands to attention, and that is the violent communiqué which Giovanni found in one of the university's Maoist sheets. He brought it to us.

On (insert date) the Glorious Cell No. 6 of the Youth Freedom Army has scored another Victory for the People, Three notorious Enemies of the People who are in Italy under the pretext of research (How many times have we heard this?) have been made to turn over 250,000 lire to our Army. We Congratulate our Comrades from the bottom of our Hearts.

Well, at least the amount was correct. Carlo hadn't made off with any of the money.

"It makes me sick," said Giovanni, "that money

given to you for your beautiful experiences should now buy guns for destruction purposes. Madmen!"

"Sex always starts wars," said Myra.

And thus, the day rolled around for our departure. In order to tidy up the sum of our experiences here, I must in all fairness mention two letters.

One was the last communiqué from Lorraine's Pop. "*You're out of the will,*" it said, starkly.

Regretfully, Lorraine tore up her response. The many-zippered recesses of her coats now contained only matter pertaining to her present life: money, combs, hairpins, addresses, cigarettes and a few assorted pills.

The other letter was from Dr. Kaminski, a letter which I know only parts of since Myra tactfully censored some of it. The professor thanked his wife for her last letter and said that the whole department was vitally interested in our trip. He thanked me also for the progress of our journey and the help I gave Myra in locating the backbone of his theory. He also described some of the life back on campus. The kids were okay, the new secretary, Lolita, was working out just fine and V. Torso was, as usual, full of misplaced venom, while Dr. Collins left much of the departmental affairs in the professor's hands. Naturally, he missed his wife and so on.

This letter awoke two reactions in me. On the one hand, I would have liked to pretend that I didn't give a damn; on the other, I felt a little guilty, as if it had been me who had taken Myra from her family. How unfounded this last feeling was can be seen simply by checking on the beginnings of this journey. Myra had been suggested to *me*, not vice versa. I was, undoubtedly, part of the plan.

Several times I tried to engage Myra on this subject, but she was curt and mysterious. I didn't worry. She was a grown woman, she knew what she was doing.

Not so Lorraine. The young *bella* had fallen head over heels in love with Italy, Roma and the rest. It was painful having to pack her bags. Did you ever notice how conservative youth really is?

We were seen off by a grand entourage of all our new friends. We were flying to Paris, a city designated as our next stop by the kind Jesuit Father Benedetti, who did not read the gossip sheets and who had called us with the invaluable information that the chalice we had been so interested in was definitely in France. Beyond that, however, the good father knew nothing.

EIGHT

As the plane swooped down on Orly, which was
under military guard on account of a terrorist attack,
the third Scotch of the trip warmed me considerably.
The pilot said that it was a mellow day in Paris, a
beautiful spring day, and that we could land as soon
as the terrorists had been rounded up, which could
be in ten minutes or six weeks. The Seine, seen from
the air, made little loops of hope.

We did land. In six minutes.

Monsieur Jerome was extremely polite. Around sixty,
he carried the weight of his ecclesiastically soft body
through the venerable air of his library like a young
tiger.

"During the war," said Monsieur, caressing an old
book with long, elegant fingers, "a miracle happened

in Loire. A gold chalice appeared on the altar of the cathedral there. It was a pagan cup engraved with orgiastic Greek scenes. The priest, dear old Father Bourget, God rest his soul, saw the obscene engraving as an allegory of the Occupation and of the terrible times we were then living under. Thousands of people came to see it. The German Kommandatur then confiscated the chalice and, since then, all efforts to locate it have been in vain. My dear friend Captain LaCrosse of the French police has been on this case since 1944. He may be able to supply you with some information. Unfortunately, good old Father Bourget's strict morals kept him from describing the cup in any helpful measure."

We thanked Monsieur and walked softly out of the majestic old house. We strolled up the tree-shaded avenue. It was an ancient street of Paris, strewn with beautiful mansions bordering their walled-in gardens on each other.

Lorraine turned to me. "Do you believe in this cup?"

I scratched my head. "One thing is for sure. If it exists, it must be quite something."

"It exists," said Myra. "Theocritus of Syracuse, Adeus of Macedon, Asclepius of Samos, Callimachus of Cyrene and Philostrates all speak of it."

"Well, if those guys do ..." said Lorraine, "I'm impressed."

Myra went on, "Greece is so perfect, so divine, so perverse."

"I must be a jerk," said Lorraine. "I'm just horny. And hungry, too."

We left for dinner and an evening of food and other satisfactions. Throughout dinner, which was superb (vichyssoise, lobster and flan), I couldn't shake the curious feeling that, in spite of our travels through the modern world, we were, in fact, visiting Ancient Greece. Myra's continuous explications of the time and circumstances of the phantom-chalice transported us to a time of magic and bacchanalia.

At the hotel, Lorraine swigged her champagne in Myra's lap and lapsed into an enthusiastic soliloquy while I tried to take some notes for my Great Story. Myra looked absentmindedly at the neon lights of Paris, her eyes looking through time at some indescribable Greek scene, half-listening to Lorraine.

"Just think! At this very moment, back in Dubuque, my school chums are leafing through the graduation album. They stop to look at my picture and say: 'There always was something weird about that gal!' Then they close the book and run to the horrible smell in the kitchen: "I've burned the damn casserole again!"

One thing's for sure, I wrote in my notes, *we are pretty far from Dubuque.*

The afternoon had been set aside for meeting Captain Jean-Pierre LaCrosse. We thus had a whole morning to waste and, frankly, this is exactly what we planned to do.

It was spring in Paris, and I was whistling the song. It will always be spring in Paris. The natives have it in them. On my grave I want inscribed the following: ROUTINE DESTROYS THE PENIS. Otherwise, the grave shall be unmarked. I was grateful for the French kiss, French coffee, the French connection and French art.

I woke early, way before the girls, and I spent a

few delicious minutes watching the light stream in through the half-open windows with the faintly rustling curtains, listening to the incredible noises of early-morning Paris: sharp voices, the clink of coffee cups, a few stray cars, the first stirrings of a great city.

From the window, my gaze wandered to my two naked beauties sharing the vast satin cage in the middle of the room. The width of the thing defied the imagination. It must have belonged to a grand duchess. Its four bronze posts on which a baroque sculptor had lavished an unending stream of plump angels and curiously twisted leaves supported it with a kind of triumphant impunity, like Hercules carrying off a young girl.

Lorraine had somehow, during the night, thrown off most of her covers, which ended up covering her head but not much else. She was stretched out in the most curious formation imaginable. One of her slender legs rested on a book Myra had been reading before going to bed, called *The Indexed Myth of Persephone,* opened on a page of illustrations showing a diagram of an ancient temple. Her other leg was dangling out of bed on my side.

Myra was stretched out full length on her back, covered to the navel by the satin coverlets. Her full, ripe breasts rose and fell with her breath, and her nipples, for some reason, were erect. The two of them formed a human configuration not much unlike the picture of the temple in the book. Like a timid worshipper I planted myself in a hollow between Lorraine's left foot and Myra's breasts and I began to concentrate intensely on their bodies, feeling a wave of desire rise within and without me. With the lightest possible touch, I brushed Lorraine's thigh with one finger almost to the opening of her full blond mound. I repeated this action several times. She didn't wake up.

Next I moved left with my finger, like a monk perusing as ancient manuscript, and traced the shape of Myra's left breast with it. She stirred a bit, half-aroused by some obscure dream which was beginning to come true.

My finger rested lightly on her nipple. I bent over Lorraine, and I rested my lips on her left breast. A little time passed, during which I could feel distinctly that, even though far from awake, the girls had begun having definite dreams of delicious indulgence. On the wake of this feeling, I became bolder and took Lorraine's whole breast—or almost—in my mouth, resting my tongue on her now definitely erect raisin. My hand cupped Myra's at the same time and lightly massaged it. I felt as if, on the flying pillows of an Oriental potentate, I was about to float through the air.

Abruptly, but still not awake, Lorraine jerked one leg up off the book, and her knee dangled to one side. This offered a whole new position and direction to the configuration in the bed, and I took appropriate steps by navigating downward between her legs and kissing, barely, her nether lips. A small frill of love-wetness greeted the touch.

We smoked some cigarettes in bed, spilled the ash-tray, called for breakfast and devoured the croissants and greedily sipped the coffee, feeling light and very happy. The incredible French street below had now filled with a cacophony of energetic sounds. We idly listened to it, barely conscious of time.

This morning everyone took about only a second to dress, a definite improvement from other mornings when a half hour, for Lorraine, could be called rapid.

When the boy came with the telegrams, we were just about out the door. Paolo Lars in Rome: CASTING ALMOST COMPLETED. AWAITING THE NEXT INSTALLMENT. MARIA LEONE DEFINITELY CHERRY. A third yet came from Maria Leone for Lorraine: DEAR CHERRY, THE CHERRIES ARE IN BLOOM, (signed) CHERRY.

We embarked on our walk. What surrealism! I thought. Somewhere in Rome, there were people who awaited the next installment of our lives (the scene this morning, perhaps) in order to imitate it on the screen for people who might be interested in forgetting their own lives for the sake of ours. Most curious!

"What's the next installment, Cherry?" I asked Lorraine, who had hastily zipped her lettergram in one of her labyrinthine pockets.

"The next installment is SHOPPING! It's getting too warm for leather. I have to get something silky, springy, frilly and frivolous."

"Yeah," Myra warmed to the idea, "something Belle Epoque. Some hats with ribbons."

We hit the stores and began to rapidly get weighted down by beautiful, pastel-colored dresses with ruffles, hats with ribbons and, for my own passage to spring, a wide-lapeled beige suit. The shop responsible for most of this was selling the spring collection of Monsieur Barzin, just shown at Versailles.

"It seems to me that our journey will become something completely different if Creghi publishes it in a Communist newspaper," said Myra.

"How so?"

"Well, obviously they aren't going to go for the human side of these capitalist monsters who flit through Europe having a good time ... stealing unique national treasures while trying out the beds in fancy hotels...."

"Decadent pirate imperialists," said Lorraine, who, back in Michigan, had briefly attended a Socialist meeting where the above phrase remained with her.

"Exactly."

"It doesn't help our search for the cup," Myra said thoughtfully. "They'll hound us if they find out where we are."

"Great, then we can go around in disguises and break into museums at night...."

"Yeah, sure, Lorraine."

It was now 12:30 A.M., still incredibly early, and Myra had a date at the Bibliothèque Nationale to rummage through a certain archive. Our meeting with Captain LaCrosse was at 4 P.M. in the café on Place Pigalle. Lorraine and I would meet her there.

Lorraine wanted to go gargoyle-hunting, and, as everyone knows, Paris is a gargoyle hunter's Mecca. The cornices of every building display gargoyles. It's like watching a convention of fantastic beings, Lorraine told me after a while. Unfortunately, she said, gargoyles quit talking when you look at them. It is a little like surprising someone at a party who just happens to be talking about your boyfriend.

And in this manner, with our heads in the clouds, we made our way toward Place Pigalle.

The café was crowded. Myra wasn't there yet, so we took a table and sat down to wait. As we looked around, no one in the room fit our image of a policeman. Perhaps he was late too.

Suddenly, Lorraine said: "I don't think I'm suitably dressed. I have the feeling this cop is very proper. I'll see you later." And she bounded out of the café. I looked after her, then I shrugged my shoulders and took a sip of my café au lait.

Myra was very late. She came in, looking worried and excited as she pushed her way to my table. "Something came up...." she was saying, but before she could finish, a cold voice interrupted: "Hope I am not too late!"

Standing there was a pale and distinguished gentleman in an expensively tailored suit. Elegant ebony glasses perched lightly on his nose. Behind them, a knotted black line of eyebrows outlined two cold blue eyes.

"Captain LaCrosse, Brandon Stone."

"You can call me Jean-Pierre!" the captain assured me. But something about him was not very reassuring.

He sat down. "Are you enjoying your stay?"

"Yes, France has been good to us," I said.

"This is a particularly good café," LaCrosse said. "I watch my favorite whores here."

Myra smiled. "What are the police attitudes toward prostitution in France?"

"Police attitudes, madame, are eternal police attitudes. Now my personal attitudes range from exultation to...."

At this point, LaCrosse half-turned and watched intently as two young hookers paced back and forth in front of the café, then turned and came in, their high heels clicking on the parquet, fur collars raised and nylons split by a neat black line at the back.

"The blonde one is Monique," said LaCrosse. "The brunette is Colline."

But, of course, I knew them already. They had been at the party at my friend Ron's antiques warehouse on my last night in San Francisco. A fortuitous meeting! But Myra interrupted before I could call to them.

"What do you propose we research next?" she asked the captain. "There seems to be a consensus that the chalice is in France."

"You are certainly aware, Madame Kaminski, that even though the case of the Loire cup is officially closed, information regarding it is still confidential."

"Have you abandoned hope of finding it, Monsieur LaCrosse?"

"Personally, yes. But the cup belongs to France, and all leads are carefully traced."

"Is it possible that the cup was taken to Germany by the SS?"

"No," he said sternly.

"Where should we begin?"

"I would begin by searching out witnesses to the miracle and comparing their necessarily blurred memories with the picture of the chalice you are seeking. I must congratulate you, Dr. Kaminski, on discovering the similarity between the Persephone cup and the so-called Loire cup. It is a pity we did not have a scholar of your caliber during the original investigation. I have here a file of names and addresses. These people were questioned a number of times. You are welcome to try again." LaCrosse unzipped a small leather case and took out a sheet of paper. "Names and addresses. Ten years old, I might add."

At this moment I caught Monique's eye. The two of them had taken a table to the left of us. LaCrosse had his back to them. I motioned her over, but Monique pointed to the captain's back and signaled silence.

"Pardon me, I must go to the bathroom," I said, I headed toward the back of the café. Monique got up casually and went in the same direction. We met on the small vestibule in the back in front of MESSIEURS and MADAMES.

"How nice to see you!" she said. "Do you know who you are sitting with?"

"Captain LaCrosse?"

"Not just Captain LaCrosse, dear. That's de Sade LaCrosse, as the girls call him."

"Really?"

"Oh-la-la!" said Monique, "We must not be seen now."

"Where could we meet?"

She scribbled an address on a napkin.

When I returned, I found Myra and LaCrosse conducting a learned discussion about the Greek origin of the chalice and the possible significance of the erotic figures on it. The captain's image of the Loire cup was remarkably like the faded picture we had discovered in the Vatican. It was, undoubtedly, the same object.

"I must hurry now," the captain said and, with a polite farewell, he walked through the door, his severe silhouette slowly vanishing across the square.

"Well, *mon ami*, we are in for tremendous intrigue," Myra said after he was gone. "I don't know if we should stay or run away as fast as possible."

"Let's hear it."

"It all begins in Loire. The commandant of the SS detail there during the Occupation was a certain General Johannes Peter von Krantz." Myra looked at me expectantly.

"What's that mean?"

"That means, in plain French, Jean-Pierre LaCrosse."

I laughed. "That's stupid. Nobody would last under such transparent cover. Besides, there are witnesses.... It's absurd.

"It's absurd, precisely."

"Even so, suppose the two captains are the same, what's that got to do with the cup?"

"*O simplicimus!* That means LaCrosse has the cup!"

"Just like that! LaCrosse has the cup!"

Back at the hotel, Lorraine was reading movie magazines.

"Why can't I be in the movie of my life?" she pouted when she saw us. "I'm as pretty as Maria Leone, and I can act."

"Something came up, Lorraine. Things might get strange." I told her of Myra's suspicion.

Lorraine absorbed the information with eyes full of wonder. "That's fantastic! Do you think LaCrosse has our cup?"

"Not *our* cup." Myra corrected her.

"I have an idea!"

I had had enough of ideas for one day. But Lorraine insisted: "He doesn't know me, right?"

"Right."

"Well, then, I can pose as a prostitute and enter the inner sanctum!"

All efforts to dissuade her were in vain. We decided to give Lorraine's plan a try.

"Not like that, for goodness' sake, *pour la mére de Dieu!*" exclaimed Monique, annoyed.

Lorraine flushed. She was wearing nylons, high-heeled shoes and an ungodly amount of lipstick and was taking the Monique *et* Colline Elementary Hooker Course.

Three days later she took her first walk. Colline had carefully put the word out that there was a smashing new American on the rack. Monsieur LaCrosse was the first to come down and have a look.

Myra and I sat nervously by the telephone that evening, waiting for the network of prearranged signals to start functioning. Monique and Colline were to stay with Lorraine at all times, and they were to try to accompany her inside the captain's house under the pretext of watching over her novitiate. If they were unsuccessful they were to call us immediately and I would sit watch in front of the house. If two hours later Lorraine had not emerged I was to go in. It I didn't come out Myra was to call the police and Monsieur Jerome.

"That tiny camera was a stupid idea," said Myra. "He won't let her out of his sight."

We waited and waited. Finally, the phone rang. It was Lorraine.

"Phew!" she said.

"How did it go?"

"I'll be home in a few minutes. As soon as I find a taxi. You won't believe it!"

Relieved, we started on champagne.

The phone rang again. Myra picked it up. "Hello? Paolo? Now?! I'm eating. I know it's your money I'm eating. No. Lorraine isn't here. When? I don't know. Call again tonight. The Communists? No, Paolo, I don't have the popularized version. That's Lorraine's specialty. Okay, *ciao*, Paolo."

"What the hell was that?"

"Paolo wanted new adventures. The Communists are interested."

We went back to the champagne.

"You didn't ask him if the Communists were going to give the story a slant, did you?"

"No. Why? Of course they will. There is nothing we can do about that. I hope the movie will be slightly more accurate."

I laughed, "You're kidding. I can just see Maria Leone putting a letter from her father in the pocket of her *zippered* jacket...."

Myra laughed too. There was, indeed, something incongruous about the elegant Maria Leone changing into a mischievous American schoolgirl.

"Where is she?" It seemed a long time since Lorraine's call. I glanced anxiously at the clock. Over an hour had gone by.

"We don't all have to go to Loire," Myra said. "Either you or I could go and check LaCrosse's list...."

"I will go," I said.

There hadn't been a sign from Monique and Colline. Myra and I made small talk. I was beginning to get an icy feeling in the pit of my stomach.

When Lorraine finally came in, two hours later, she could hardly walk. She stumbled to the bed and lay on it. We gave her a drink.

"Look," she said before she passed out. In the bed next to her she flung a handful of photographs.

NINE

"This is the sitting room," explained Lorraine. "It is the only room I was alone in for a few minutes."

This sitting room was a largely rococo environment, airy and vast. The walls were covered with paintings, and the desks accommodated a number of miniatures as well as a disarray of books and prints. The room was festooned with art. With a magnifying glass we made out a print of *Satan and His Followers* by Henri de Malrost, possibly an illustration from the notorious *Le Satanisme et la magie*, by Jules Bois, Paris, 1895. The devil, handsome as you please, sat atop a hill with a mask over his genitals while an endless row of humans filed by touching the mask with their outstretched fingers. The two girls at the head of the column, who had already touched the mask, were poised to walk into a gold bathtub.

A little out of focus, Jean Bourdichon's *St. Sebastian* peered from the wall with an array of wounds. A delicately framed miniature of damned priests from a fourteenth-century edition of Dante's *Inferno* proved the old adage: Hell Is Fun.

Until this time I had always believed that all that remained of Gilles de Rais had been the ruins at Machecoul, but a crude medieval drawing, photographed at an angle by Lorraine, showed Joan of Arc receiving instruction from the notorious Bluebeard for whom she had burned at the stake.

"It is beyond belief!" said Myra. "This is all stuff stolen from European museums during the war. The Henri de Malrost used to be in the Louvre."

"So that's the sitting room. What was the rest?"

Here Lorraine had to rely on memory, and she was visibly shaken trying to remember.

"It was big. The walls were cherry-satined, and things hung from them. All kinds of chains and rings covered with velvet. He asked me to undress...."

After undressing, Lorraine stood there in the middle of the room, waiting for the captain, who was appraising her severely, to do something. He looked at the clothes which Lorraine, for lack of a chair, had merely dumped on the floor. Then he asked her to step through a low wooden door.

"I was getting a little spooked by the man.... I mean, there he was, looking at me with those cold blue eyes like someone examining an insect, and then he tells me to go through that door.... I felt really humiliated, I was about ready to grab my gear and sprint.... I don't know why I didn't.... I went through the door.... It was a low, heavy wooden door with metal things on it like a dungeon door or something...."

On the other side was a completely white cell, a closet-sized monk's cell with a narrow bed in it. A small barred window gave onto a cement courtyard. Everything was hospital white except a black crucifix on the opposite wall from the window, over the bed. There was no place to sit except on the bed, so Lorraine sat on it, feeling "a strange mixture of religiosity and arousal."

After what seemed like an exceedingly long time in which fear mixed with curiosity washed all over her naked body, which was, incidentally, covered with goosebumps because it was rather chilly in the cell, the dungeon door opened and Captain LaCrosse made his appearance dressed in a black priest's robe of the Inquisition.

"He looked really impressive in it.... I felt this weird terror which kind of turned me on.... I know it was a game, but I wasn't really sure.... What if, I thought, he's going to torture and kill me.... But when he got closer I realized ... well, there was a slit in the robe under the navel.... I didn't see it at first, I didn't see it until ... well, he came up to me and ordered me to kneel on the bed facing the crucifix and talk dirty to him.... Now that's not really hard.... Me and my girlfriends used to have pajama parties where we talked real dirty until we got all hot and bothered ... so I closed my eyes and I thought of being at a pajama party with Sue Ann and Betty Evans and let go this stream of filthy words. I was beginning to feel real warm all over.... After a while, I opened my eyes.... I couldn't help it ... and I saw LaCrosse in his black robe standing up with a ...

well, I've never seen, I've never even *heard of* anything like that, a giant ... and I mean *giant* prick sticking straight out of his robe.... It was incredible...."

Thereafter followed some rather conventional dialogue made complicated only by the excessive size of that organ which took some maneuvering and the captain's relentless energy, which seemed to last and last.

Judging by Lorraine's shaky condition it had been a rather unique experience.

"How did you get the pictures?"

"Well, afterward, when I was putting my clothes back on ... the camera fell out of my pocket, and LaCrosse picked it up.... He looked at it, then he looked at me and said if I had any pictures to get developed there was a place on the Boulevard St. Michel where they did them for you on the spot...."

"And you went there," I said.

"Yeah."

"Great, now he's got a set of prints...."

"Really?"

We laughed.

My rented Mercedes ate the highway flawlessly and powerfully. On the dash, LaCrosse's list fluttered in the light breeze whistling in through the half-open window. I had time to collect my thoughts.

A week had elapsed since Lorraine's adventure with LaCrosse. Four days of this week had been set aside by Myra and myself to take care of Lorraine. There wasn't anything wrong with her, per se, but she felt like being mothered. After all, she was still a child. We lavished care and affection on her. We fed her hot soup, juices, champagne and movie magazines.

I will always remember these four days affection-
ately. There was an idyllic family feeling about them.
I felt paternal and loving, and Myra was beyond herself with tenderness. In her diary, Myra said:

Lorraine is lying in bed, and mama feeds and entertains
her. It makes me want to see my daughters. Today I wrote
them a long letter. I sure hope they understand what I'm
doing. Do I understand myself?

The telephone was off the hook, the bellboy had
instructions to keep everyone out and mail from Italy
piled on an end table, unread.

I made some notes for my story, jotting down,
mainly, in various forms, the thought of my original
naiveté. How in the world, I asked myself over and
over, could I ever hope to lock a human being in a
mesh of words? My naive ambition to build a woman
in my story completely ignored the facts, which were
love, mystery, concern. Given those facts, no impris-
onment was valid.

Myra tended to her diary, writing in a kind of nos-
talgic prose her dreamlike feeling of the twist our
adventures seemed to be taking. Strewn among her
various observations were a variety of questions
regarding Captain Jean-Pierre LaCrosse.

On the fifth day we rejoined the world by making
an appointment with Monsieur Jerome. We were told
by the young Jesuit secretary that Monsieur was not
very well. But we did not expect, next morning,
when we arrived at the mansion, to find him quite so
changed.

Monsieur looked as if a sudden illness had swept
over him, rendering his svelte figure completely cav-

ernous. His cheeks were sunken, and he was confined to a wheelchair. The difference was astonishing. In the course of one week, he had been mowed down mercilessly. He noticed our astonishment.

"It is called the priests' disease here in France. It strikes one of six of us. They tell me it was visited upon us for abuse of the confessional."

"Your sense of humor is as splendid as ever, monsieur," Myra said. "I hope you will not be upset by what we are going to show you."

We showed Monsieur Jerome the photographs. He looked at them grimly, shaking his head. Pointing to *Satan and His Followers,* he said: "In number sixteen of the *Bulletin de Société Historique* for 1945, there is a story concerned with this print. It was alleged that Goebbels' agents had stolen it."

"There is no doubt," said Monsieur Jerome after identifying each picture, "that you have here a good record of satanic art stolen from France during the war.... There is more, of course."

Myra delivered the punch line: "They were photographed in the living room of Monsieur Jean-Pierre LaCrosse."

The venerable clergyman looked at us, puzzled for a moment; then the wrinkles around his mouth spread out concentrically in sudden amusement. He laughed. Briefly, his youthful vigor returned.

"You are not aware, I gather, of Jean-Pierre's method...."

"Oh, no!" I said, guessing the truth.

"Yes, indeed, he has been hunting stolen French art for three decades, and what you have photographed are clever replicas used in training agents for detection." He laughed again. "When I was a child I was given a joke book. I remember one in particular very well. A man with a knife runs down the street. A policeman follows him with his gun drawn. Around the corner is a man who sharpens knives, and the 'criminal' gives it to him."

Monsieur Jerome laughed some more.

"There is something else," Myra said. "Are you aware, monsieur, that General Johannes Peter von Krantz of the SS in Loire and Captain Jean-Pierre LaCrosse have the same name?"

Monsieur looked at her impatiently. "Madame Kaminski, everyone in France knows the story. During the Resistance, Jean-Pierre was assigned to the assassination of General von Krantz. His name then used to be Jean-Pierre Laffite. When he killed von Krantz, he took on his name in accordance with an ancient custom of war, a gallant Gallic custom …" Monsieur looked very tired. "Is there anything else?"

"I don't think so…." murmured Myra.

"Very well then, I must retire."

The haughty secretary wheeled Monsieur out of the room to his bed, where he died a few days later.

I nearly swerved off the road. A rabbit. After that visit, we decided that LaCrosse was, after all, a decent fellow if a bit on the weird side, and I started for Loire to search for witnesses to the wartime miracle. I had no idea how I would go about it, but I planned, when I got to town, to pay first of all a prolonged visit to the cathedral where all this had occurred. I had seen a number of pictures of it, and I was looking forward to it. I also liked being alone for a time.

The cathedral, a splendid upward thrust of Gothic lust, towered over the town, completely disdainful of the newer modern towers rising at the edge of the city. It was a monumental stone structure crafted with the unbelievable patience of four hundred years of work. Begun in 1205, it had finally been built by 1605, just in time to be burned almost to the ground by a group of Crusaders. Rebuilt in 1630–1635, it never rose to its previous majesty, but it preserved the massive air of authority and knowledge which its builders had invested it with.

The second the cathedral appeared in my windshield I knew that the town as such existed only as a background to it, a kind of stage prop to be brought in when it needed rebuilding. And I sensed also, hidden behind those thick walls, a kind of solution to my mystery.

There was, in the magic of pushing open such a magnificent door, the eerie feeling of the suspension of time. How such a big door could slide so noiselessly and open into such a different world from the street baffled me. I had gone in through a side door which was unlocked, and I found myself in what must have been the oldest and the darkest corner of the church, a place dominated by an extremely Gothic St. Sebastian, fantastically tall, skinny and white, on whose body red blood drops fell with an exquisite certainty from his arrow wounds. There was no worshiper in sight, and the vast altar, blazing in the distance, had no one to attend it.

I could see very well how a miracle may have taken place here during the Occupation. I could almost visualize a beautiful Greek gold cup rising from that altar to shoot forth visions of a sensual paradise. It made sense. The church had been *built* to host miracles. The men who made it lived in a miraculous time, and they fervently hoped that it would be *their* church to host future miracles. This desire was written in every cornice, every window, and emanated from the altar. It was a magnificent tempting of chance. The greatest order.

During this reverie, a hand found its way on my shoulder. A middle-aged priest stood there with an incredibly mean expression on his pudgy face.

"Forgive me," I said, "I came in by the side door."

"This part of the church is closed at the moment. But if you would like confession, I will be glad to perform."

"Thank you very much, monsieur. I am Brandon Stone, from the University of Michigan. I would like to speak to the cathedral custodian."

"Our cathedral has no custodian. It is not a historical monument, it is a place of worship. We discourage archaeological digs."

"You misunderstand me, Father. I am not a historian, I am a religious scholar. I would like to know about the Miracle of the Cup."

I put up in the hotel to wait for a call from the diocese next morning. I took a shower and looked out the window. A big café on the corner was doing a booming business. I dressed and sprinted downstairs.

Seated at the next table, touching on mine from the left, were two young coquettes. The rest of the place was crowded with an assortment of thoughtful people. It is a fantastic thing for people to do their thinking in cafés. In reality, I suspected, everyone was just horny as hell and looking thoughtful was as good a way as any to appear interesting. I ordered a Pernod.

Myra and Lorraine had finished their meal, and, through the refracted glow on their champagne glasses, they set themselves to studying the surroundings. Two interesting-looking gentlemen were seated to their right. It is unclear who made the first overture, but one hour later we see them seated at the same table. To take this an hour further is to see the four laughing people come out of a taxi in front of a new apartment building. Two hours from now is to light on a feast of bodies and textures occupying the entire surface of a deep Persian rug.

I wasn't doing badly myself. I was a little weary from the exertions of the night, and my palms exposed a variety of stigmata known as "sheet burns." When the telephone call came at noon I was ready, however, and, getting my pad and pencil, I made for the cathedral.

The book-lined study was built to match the facial features of the wizened old man who was wheeled in by a priest; it was a strange room indeed. Paintings of an obscure origin representing the keepers of the church adorned its narrow length.

Without a handshake, the old priest informed me that he was a young choirboy at the time of the miracle but that every time he tries to think of what was on the cup his memory fails him. He remembered only the shape of it. He drew it. It was the shape familiar by now.

Then something extraordinary happened. The younger priest came within an inch of my face and said: "Sometimes he remembers."

"When?"

"On Great Friday of every year."

I think Monsieur was putting me on. In any case, I found out nothing more in that room. It had been a terribly staged event for some reason.

The next two days I tried to contact people on LaCrosse's list. The only person who hadn't moved or died was a charming little old lady who moved with difficulty among an extraordinary quantity of stuffed dogs and porcelain statuettes. "The miracle gave me six teeth," she said, "six new teeth...." Outside of that, she only wanted to talk about her pooch, Sylvestre, who nestled in her lap in a cloud of perfumed ribbons.

The drive back was longer.

At the Security Council, which is what we called our little conference back in Paris, Lorraine was of the opinion that we should give up looking for the phantom cup and should, instead, go to an exotic Mediterranean country to sunbathe nude on the beach. But Myra was obsessed:

"The cup is around. I can just feel it. At this point, I cannot let my husband down. In his last letter, he was so excited by our apparent proximity to the chalice, he said it gave new meaning to his life...."

"We are at a dead end, Myra. LaCrosse was on the level.... There was nothing in Loire...." I was inclined to side with Lorraine.

Myra was on the verge of tears. "Why don't you two just go? I'll stay here and do what I have to do...."

"What do you want to do?" I asked her.

"Go myself to Loire, search out more witnesses,

spend my time at the *bibliothèque*, study every lead...."

"It could take a thousand years!" Lorraine too was upset.

"It might be a game to you ..." Myra said to her in a voice so unlike her I was startled. "... to me it's important! You can go to hell if you want! Go to Italy and float in that hussy's bathtub if you want!"

"Now, wait just a minute!" Lorraine stomped her foot on the soft carpet. "I have a right to my affairs!"

Myra picked her diary book off the table and put it under her arm. She left the room.

"Myra loves you," I said to Lorraine. "She thinks you don't care for her. You're always in the clouds somewhere, playing. Doesn't anything upset you?"

"I'm upset right now. It's not that I don't love her.... I'm mad about her, and she knows it. It's just that I don't give a fig about this cup. Neither do you, really."

I admitted it. "Maybe not. But I love Myra, and I think we should respect her position. Remember our original purpose."

"Original purpose be damned! Myra can't make up her mind if she wants me or the cup!"

"You'd force her to make a choice?" I was shocked.

"Yes, I would. And what's more, you'll have to make a choice too. I'm going to the Riviera tomorrow!"

Myra pursued the argument in her diary, sitting by herself at a café a few streets from the hotel:

The cup is my only defense against any further involvement with Lorraine. It's mad, this thing between women.

*Taking care of her like a child for a few days, then getting
into an orgy two days later, wham-bang, it's a kaleidoscope
of feelings. I've got a soft spot for the kid, no question
about it. Brandon is like a juggler. He keeps the balance
between us as if it's a circus act for his—Great Story. I
must decide now: Am I a fool or a scientist?*

She whistled the first few bars of "What a Fool am I":
"What a fool am I/Ever since your good-bye...."

Evening was well advanced when Myra returned.
Colline and Monique had arrived a few minutes
before to pay us a surprise visit. Clutching her notebook like a schoolgirl and without greeting any of us,
Myra walked softly into the room, grabbed a half-full
bottle of champagne, and locked herself in the bathroom. We heard the shower.

"Ah!" said Colline. "A domestic battle!"

"A *fronde!*" said Monique.

Myra came out with a towel wrapped around her
waist and, without greeting the assembled company,
threw herself on the bed face down on a copy of *The
Life and Times of an Involuntary Genius*, a book she had
bought in Italy allegedly written by a Rumanian
anarchist. She obviously preferred his company to
ours.

"We were just leaving," said Monique.

"But we just arrived," Colline protested.

"Well, what's the night life like in Paris? My last
walk cured me for a while," said Lorraine.

"Ah! It seems that no one is sleeping at night anymore!" said Monique.

"Everybody is awake," said Colline. "Ohlala!"

"It's the fault of television," I said.

"Yes," Monique said, cupping her breasts with

both hands and holding them up to the light, "A very old television."

"We are the first TV!" said Colline proudly.

"I thought water was," I said.

"I have to go pee-pee," said Monique.

"Not me," said Colline. "I drink Diet-Cola."

At this point, Myra, who was pretending not to hear, took her eyes off the Rumanian anarchist, looked at the girls and began laughing. We joined in. We laughed for an hour.

After Monique and Colline left, Myra tried to ignore us again, but she wasn't mad anymore. She had a hard time keeping a straight face.

But Lorraine wasn't in a funny mood any longer. "What did you decide?" she asked Myra.

"I haven't decided yet."

"Tell her, Brandon," Lorraine said to me.

"Tell her yourself."

"Okay. I want to go to the Riviera *tomorrow*...."

Myra didn't say anything.

Next morning, bright and early, Lorraine sprinted out of bed and threw her new collection of frills and ruffles into a suitcase. Myra woke up and watched her from the bed with her arms under her head. I got up.

"You're serious. Are you going to Nice?"

"Nice, Deauville, I don't care."

"Maybe we will go...."

Myra said nothing. Lorraine stopped packing and looked at us for a moment. "I'm going out for coffee. I'll be back in about an hour.... I hope you have made up your minds by then."

She left.

Myra and I looked at each other. "Whoosh!

Whoosh!" said Myra, imitating with her hand a severe spanking.

I was in complete agreement. "Whoosh, whoosh!" I said, adding my open palm to Lorraine's imaginary ass.

"Do you think she's spoiled?"

"Rotten," said Myra Kaminski, Ph.D.

"What are we going to do?"

"Speak for yourself."

"What are you going to do?"

"Give me a massage, Brandon. I can think better that way." Myra turned over. I appraised her graceful back running curvilinearly over her ass to the juncture of her thighs, where a reddish tuft of hair was barely visible. The line ran unbroken over her thighs to the long, elegant toes. I sat on her ass and began with her neck. I was conscientiously massaging her, feeling her pliant muscles underneath, releasing the tension. But as I began to approach her ass my hands began another sort of movement which, while not strictly part of an orthodox massage, was related to it in subtle ways. I kneaded her ass cheeks. There was no tension in them whatsoever. From there I caressed her thighs, hesitating by the red tuft of hair. My hand sank lower. She was wet.

I regained my original position, but this time I could feel beads of sweat forming, moistening the head of my searching party. I made love to her with slow, long strokes.

Afterward, lying there, completely, blissfully semiconscious, I wondered for a second where Lorraine was. But I felt sleepy and, at first, I had a long reverie in which a gold Aztec god kept waving at a department vestal virgin as she rounded the corner of the temple to get some candles, but then I drifted into real sleep and into an office where Myra and Lorraine were filling in forms to change their names officially to Mrs. and Mrs. Brandon Stone, but then we had a quarrel about the wedding and didn't do it.

I woke up soon enough, and I saw that I was alone. There was a note on the dresser. WENT TO LOOK FOR CHERRY AT THE CAFÉS. YOU SNORE. LENORE

I must have been sleeping for a long time. It was already ten o'clock. I showered, shaved, put on some clean clothes. I was feeling pretty good, really. I thought the whole situation was silly. If Lorraine goes to the Riviera by herself, then we'll just have to join her when she gets lonely. But, of course, if we all went, it would be so much better. I saw us lying on the white sands of the beach under an umbrella and at our feet the Mediterranean. Oh, I loved Capri and Naples! Paris, by contrast, was hot, sticky and weird. I wanted to go.

I opened all the windows and let the sunshine in. It was a fairly cool day, but there wasn't a single cloud in the sky. It would get hotter. I felt like going swimming.

The hotel had a swimming pool, so I ordered breakfast to be brought to the side of it and went in for a dip. I left a note for Myra and Lorraine, if they returned.

I devoured the eggs Benedict and the side order of asparagus, drank my coffee at leisure and watched the water ripple in the multicolored skylight.

Hours later they had still not come back, so I went looking for them, leaving a third note: WENT LOOKING FOR YOU. LET'S EAT AT MAXIM'S TONIGHT. JACK SCOTT.

I tried about a dozen cafés before I gave up. In the last one, on Rue Durant, I had a Pernod. The room looked like a striped cage of sunlight, and the bored monsieur behind the counter was asleep in last night's edition of *France Soir*. Yes, we must leave Paris. Summer is unbearable in a city, even the greatest on earth. I noted with irony how much my tastes had changed since I ran into money. If I wanted to go someplace now, I could just pick up and go. Being poor is definitely boring.

Suddenly Myra appeared and sat down just as if this meeting had been prearranged weeks ago.

"Did you find Lorraine?" I asked.

"No, did you?"

"Not a trace. She must've skipped town."

We walked back to the hotel, where we immediately noticed Lorraine's half-packed suitcase. "She wouldn't leave without clothes," Myra said.

"She can buy new ones. Besides, all she needs is a bikini."

"Okay, Brandon," Myra said, "I'll tell you what. Let's stay in Paris for two more days so I will be positive that no new information on the chalice exists. Then we'll go follow Lorraine to the Riviera."

I thought that was reasonable.

We had dinner at Maxim's and came home around eleven that night, slightly tipsy. Lorraine still hadn't returned.

As I was struggling to get out of my clothes I noticed that the bag Lorraine usually carried, a Moroccan pouch, was on the floor. I picked it up. All of Lorraine's stuff was inside, including her passport and all her money.

"Myra! Either she's back or something weird's going on. She doesn't have a penny."

A horrible thought crossed both our minds. I easily imagined Lorraine kidnapped. Bound and gagged. Or worse.

Neither of us could sleep. We stayed up waiting for her like two solicitous parents. When neither the phone nor the door budged, we decided it was time to act. We called LaCrosse.

We woke him up. He was sleepy. "What can I do for you?"

"I know this isn't the hour, monsieur, but our companion Lorraine disappeared and we believe something happened to her. Can you help us?"

He woke at once and laughed. "Is this a joke? A revenge for the petite *chouchou?*"

Myra assured him that it was not.

"I will be there in twenty-five minutes," he said.

He came in, impeccably dressed, a half-hour later.

"How long has she been gone?" he asked.

"I know it sounds silly, but only since this morning."

The captain feigned indignation. "You got me out of bed for this?"

We explained the circumstances. She didn't have a penny.

LaCrosse looked at us like a severe pedagogue would look at two wayward children. "I will alert the police. But frankly, between us, I think she probably has a taste for the Paris night life...."

I pretended to be surprised.

"There is no need to pretend with me," said LaCrosse. "Her photographs of my living room were terrible."

"That was an odd idea of Lorraine's, monsieur. I hope you are not angry. The main thing now is to find her...."

"Yes, of course," he obliged us. "It could be serious."

Though he wasn't much help, for the moment the captain's visit had reassured us a little. Perhaps she would be back in the morning.

But she wasn't. Or the next morning for that matter.

TEN

The woman sat on a stump watching Lorraine wash her hair in the cold mountain stream. All around them, the fir forest extended to the horizon. The woman watched her intently with a kind of puzzlement. Her face, which was that of a handsome young Italian woman in her late twenties, was extremely serious and determined. Her long black hair was drawn back tightly in a bun. Her breasts were large, with well-formed nipples. The camouflage jacket she wore was unbuttoned, and she wore no shirt. At her feet lay a small Chinese-made machine gun.

Lorraine squeezed the last drop of water from her hair and asked the woman for a comb. Obligingly, the guerrilla rummaged through the sagging pockets of her fatigue jacket and came up with an ebony comb.

"Can you comb it?" said Lorraine easily, sitting at her feet, careful not to touch the weapon.

The woman hesitated for a second, looked intently at Lorraine, who was a picture of innocence and unconcern, and thrust the comb into Lorraine's blonde mane. With her foot she pushed the gun to her left.

"Flora!" A man stood there, leaning against a tree. "She can comb her own hair!"

"Can you?" asked Flora.

"No," said Lorraine, shaking her wet head, "it's a mess!"

Flora combed her hair. The man, whose name was Che, watched them and said nothing.

Seeing Maria Leone again was pleasant, even under the understandably tense circumstances. Her limousine had whisked us up from the airport straight to her house. She was indeed beautiful. I had forgotten just how beautiful. Her black almond eyes were set in her oval face like two magnetic stars. She embraced us over and over, crying and laughing at the same time. "We will get her back, I swear we will. If it costs me my whole fortune!"

Giovanni Creghi, Paolo Lars, Alonso and a squat dark man in a business suit were waiting for us in a small drawing room.

"These have been some days," said Paolo, after we were all seated comfortably around a small table on Turkish footstools.

The squat man who had been introduced as Signor Giacomo went straight to the heart of the matter: "What concerns us now is whether we can fulfill the terrorist demand or not."

"Well," said Paolo, "it's absolutely preposterous. Are you sure we cannot offer them money?"

"In my experience," Signor Giacomo said, "terrorists have extraordinary reasons for their actions. I would not try to continue negotiations. We risk losing communication."

"In that case we must find a way."

"Precisely."

The present company perused once again the last communiqué from the Youth Freedom Army, analyzing every word, looking for other possible interpretations. There were none. The document stated clearly:

Our terms for the girl's release are as follows. One: The YFA demands one of the three starring roles in the movie to be produced by Paolo Lars about the American sex team. Two: A cultural liaison of the YFA will be named by producer Lars as a production assistant during the making of the movie. This liaison will be empowered to change the script in any manner he elects in order that our aims and goals be described to the people in the clearest manner possible. Three: The last third of the movie will deal in entirety with the kidnapping of Lorraine and with the ideology of the Youth Freedom Army. Four: All royalties resulting from the eventual financial success of the movie will go to the YFA through an intermediary to be specified at a later date.

The tape from which this transcript had been made lay on the coffee table on top of the small Sony. On the same tape was Lorraine's voice. Lorraine said, after the above:

"Hi, lovers! You heard the story: They want to make the movie and get the dough. I have also been told that I will not be released until the movie has been distributed and international rights sold. I love you both."

There had been three of these tapes since that morning in Paris when, very early, we were awakened by a telephone call from Rome.

It was Maria Leone. In a voice trembling with emotion, she said: "I received a tape this morning. Lorraine has been kidnapped."

With our ears glued to the receiver, Myra and I listened to the incredible recording. A woman's voice, speaking a clipped Italian, said the following:

On July second, Revolutionary Unit Number Six of the Youth Freedom Army arrested the youngest member of the American CIA sex team. Terms for her release will be negotiated in subsequent communications. This is Flora, Communications Secretary of the Youth Freedom Army. Victory to the people!

Flora went on the say what our crimes had been:

Lorraine, Brandon Stone and Myra Kaminski have been hired by the CIA through the offices of an American university to study the sex behavior of certain European peoples in conjunction with a Pentagon plan to sterilize vast masses in the event of a war. Overtly describing themselves as anthropologists and art historians, they are, in reality, CIA agents. The sexual behavior of the people is not for sale. Sex is a revolutionary weapon.

Here there were a few minutes of silence in which

voices came indistinctly from the background. Then Lorraine was on:

Hi, lovers! These kids mean business. They've enrolled me in reeducation. So far it's been rice and beans, but they plan to improve the menu. Generally, I'd say you ought to do what they say on account of the fact that they have one machine gun, two....

Here she must have been yanked away from the microphone because we never did learn the exact strength of that YFA unit.

"All right, I am willing to go along with it," said Paolo Lars. "Maria will continue as Cherry. We will offer them your roles; they can choose."

"I don't think this is what they have in mind," Signor Giacomo said. "They want Lorraine's role because they have her and they mean to study her."

"That's impossible," Maria said. "I've been working on it."

Paolo turned to Maria. "Take Myra Kaminski's role. We must gain time."

Myra looked embarrassed. Maria Leone's fixation was obvious. "Look, if you want me to leave the room...."

"Nonsense," said Giacomo, "life is full of bizarre situations." He looked at Myra admiringly, "I am no movie man, but I could say Mrs. Kaminski is a splendid opportunity for Maria Leone." He had his own tastes.

Maria laughed. "This is strange.... I like you, Myra. Maybe if I played you, I can imagine to myself that I had Lorraine as many times as you did...." A quiver crept into her voice. Unconsciously, she stroked her hip. Or maybe consciously. It was hard to tell.

Myra laughed too.

"Who is me?" I said, giving Maria a little time to think.

"A young actor from Bologna, Victor Borsa. I directed him in *The Flying Divan*...." Paolo said.

"Legally," interjected Alonso, "we ought to report the kidnapping to the police."

Creghi sniggered. "My dear Alonso, I think you forget you are speaking about the Italian police." He was a medium-built man with powerful shoulders, dark hair and blue eyes, looking more Irish than Italian. I liked his affable and direct manner.

"Okay," Maria said after exchanging a number of thoughtful glances with Myra, "I will be Lenore.... I wonder who the YFA will send...."

It had been a long evening. Everyone stood up to leave after it had been agreed to communicate our decision to the terrorists through an advertisement in *Il Corriere*.

"No, I will not hear of it...." said Maria. "You are going to no hotel. We must stay together, Brandon. You and Myra will have a whole wing of the house for yourselves.... My maid will cook for you."

We stayed. After everyone had left, we became sentimental.

"Poor Lorraine.... She must be going through hell," said Maria.

Myra sighed. "It's all too horrible...."

Lorraine didn't like her sleeping conditions, but she didn't feel too bad. Deep inside her something thrilled at her unexpected position. She was feeling a growing wave of excitement. True, she had been badly frightened when the men had pushed her into the car at gunpoint. Her fear became so intense, in fact, at times she wanted to scream during the long car journey, but the gag in her mouth nauseated her and she controlled herself.

Her fear diminished considerably when, after three days and nights of a bumpy car ride during which she had been so drugged she couldn't remember her name, she saw her captors face to face.

There were five of them. The three who had been waiting ran toward the car, waving their machine guns with joy. Behind them, a wooden shack stood outlined against the tall granite walls of the mountains.

Lorraine regretted not having been better at geography. She couldn't tell what mountains these were.

The shack was furnished with the bare necessities. A rack full of kitchen utensils hung from the wall. A crude wooden table spanned the whole length of the cabin. Tree stumps served for chairs. A wood stove in the corner had two burners for cooking. Two shelves, one full of cans, another full of books, completed the decor. There were no sleeping quarters in sight, but Lorraine saw a bunch of sleeping bags rolled up and propped against a wall, and she deduced that these were strewn at night on the floor. A color poster of Mao was taped over one of the two windows, making the room pretty dark even in daytime.

Shortly after her arrival, the comrades introduced themselves, and then she went to sleep with her head on the table while they talked to each other in Italian. There was Carlo, whom she had already met, a girl named Flora, a lanky, dark man who called himself

Che and her two captors: Silvio and Curtis. Curtis was American.

When she woke, she had been laid on top of a sleeping bag on the floor and a coarse blanket with holes in it covered her. It was daytime.

Carlo was the only one in the cabin. He was reading *Soul on Ice* by Eldridge Cleaver in English.

"You're awake," he said.

"You asshole," said Lorraine, her first words in four days.

The wing of Maria's house we occupied consisted of a wave of nooks and crannies created for excessive comfort and united by a deep Persian rug which ran from room to room like water. Each room had reading places, hanging plants, stained-glass windows, oval and round beds and a proliferation of mirrors. They opened into one another through arcades.

I whistled admiringly. "Whoever made this must have had a constant hard-on...." Hanging from walls, here and there, were Renaissance miniatures depicting mostly angels, muses, clouds, harps and rosy flesh tones.

Myra said sternly: "It's the ultimate bourgeois frivolity ... look at all this silk and satin...."

I looked. Silk curtains, satin bedspreads, velvet chairs. I knew now why Lorraine liked to come here...."

We fell silent. The image of Lorraine stretched in all her youthful strength among these textures aroused me. Myra flushed.

We took off our clothes and slipped under the velvet and satin (blue and gold) cover of one of the round beds. A light switch by the bed left the room in semidarkness. An oblique red light was on under a small painting of a medieval girl.

"There are a lot of things I don't understand.... How could they hope to get away with it? The movie is going to be a flop, and they will all get caught."

"It's a daring idea...." I said. "I wish I knew where they were holding her."

"Do you think all of this has to do with the cup?"

"What do you mean?"

"Well, there is this cup we are looking for. Everywhere we run into problems. Then we are put off the track completely by this kidnapping...."

"You're imagining things. The whole thing is our fault for getting involved with all that money.... We should have gone on quietly doing what we were doing...."

There was no focus to our discussion. We just couldn't sleep.

"I can't sleep," said Maria. "Do you mind if I join you?" She was standing there in a filmy gown holding a little lamp. Her body, clearly visible under the sheer material, threw shadows around the room.

"Not at all," said Myra.

She snuggled between us. I was barely touching her thigh with mine, but l could feel the warmth of her body. She turned her back to me and drew closer to Myra, who slipped an arm under her.

I tried not to move, but the short distance between Maria's buttocks and myself was bridged suddenly by my erection. I expected her, for some reason, to draw back. Instead, she pushed lightly against my member and a drop of sperm wet the silk of her chemise. But then she did draw away from me, closer to Myra. My erection lost its proudness. I drifted to sleep.

The set was astonishingly realistic. It was a foggy San Francisco day seen through the windows of an empty classroom. Victor Borsa, a young actor who didn't look anything like me (he was much handsomer, had dark hair and black eyes), walked in and looked out at Coit Tower. These were all preliminary shots. The filming proper would begin the next day, when we expected the YFA actress to appear. Originally the script had called for the camera crew to fly to San Francisco with Victor and film the beginning there. But the events had forced Paolo to film entirely at Cinecittá.

I felt eerie sitting there on the studio lot amidst a cardboard San Francisco watching the beginnings of my adventure. Myra, who was standing next to me, shook her head. "If I was a writer I would really appreciate this.... As it is, I find the whole thing very bizarre...."

"I do too," I reassured her. I would have enjoyed this a lot more, I realized, if the events hadn't been so adverse.

Signor Giacomo was watching too. "What is the true object of your research?" he asked unexpectedly.

I pretended not to hear him, watching a dolly slide by with an enormous camera on it. But Myra answered him:

"We are looking for a sacred chalice which proves a scientific theory developed by my husband...."

"Ah," said Signor Giacomo, "that is not the premise of the movie...."

"We were trying to protect the university from unwarranted publicity."

"May I ask what you are trying to prove?"

"A few years ago my husband developed a cohesive theory of human sexuality from a historical point of view. The thrust of this theory is that sexuality works historically in *peaks* and *valleys*, and that this kind of dialectic produces at certain times a synthesis of both sexual modes. This synthesis takes the form of an object which symbolically represents the union. The sacred cup of Persephone is such an object. We were trying to locate it."

Signor Giacomo stood patiently through all this, raising his eyebrow quizzically only when Myra said "peaks" and "valleys." His ironic gaze went directly to Myra's own peaks and valleys and liked what it saw in a charmingly arrogant Italian way. When she was finished he said: "You have engaged in quite a bit of detective work, I assume...."

"We sure have."

I ran down for him the history of our stay in France, dwelling at length on Captain LaCrosse.

"Very interesting.... You will excuse me, I hope. I must do some work...."

After he was gone, Myra and I looked at each other. "I think he is a very shrewd private eye," I said.

"I hope so," agreed Myra.

Blinking wearily from the bright lights, we sat on some chairs.

"Okay! Cut!" said Paolo, walking toward us. "I just received the call we were waiting for. Our new star arrives Friday."

While she was combing Lorraine's wet hair, Flora said: "You will be a very difficult character to play. I do not understand you. Are you not aware of the great social struggles going on in your own country? I was born very poor in a little village in Lombardia. When I became a student my only purpose in life was to fight for my people...."

"Sure," said Lorraine, "but there are struggles and struggles. I struggled with myself to make myself free. I think that is important. One thing is for sure though. I am not a CIA agent."

"Do you have any connections with the CIA?" said Che, who was following the conversation.

"No, I do not. My whole family is apolitical. Daddy doesn't even vote."

Sylvio came toward them. "It is time for your political reeducation class...."

"It already started," said Lorraine. She got up, took the comb out of her hair and put her shirt on.

They walked to the shack. As they had done for five days, the terrorists sat on one side of the table facing Lorraine, who sat on a stump looking at them fearlessly. They are just kids, she thought to herself, they are just like the kids at college. They are just like me. The whole thing is a charade.

"Since you insist that you and your friends are innocent of the crimes you have been charged with, I will show you that you are neither innocent nor blameless.... We will talk about sex," said Carlo.

"Why *talk* about it?" asked Lorraine.

Carlo looked at her contemptuously. "Typical petit-bourgeois mentality."

"In a world where men and women are truly equal, sex becomes a potent revolutionary weapon, and the pursuit of a better orgasm is part of the charter of human rights along with the pursuit of sexual betterment of the *entire* community...." said Flora, reciting, it seems, from a textbook in her mind.

"Well, I can't say I haven't helped a few people along.... I'm rather proud of it too.... Why, there was this kid...."

"Cut the chatter...." said Curtis. "You are an intelligent young woman, and you can't be blind to the social aspect of sexuality ..."

And so it went, day after day. Suddenly, Lorraine felt very tired. These people were made of stone. Not once, during the time she had been here, had she seen any goings-on. Beyond a certain back-slapping camaraderie, they barely touched each other.

But later that same night things changed. She had barely laid out her sleeping bag in the darkness at the foot of the table when she felt one of the men walking toward her. He sat next to her and caressed her hair. She fought an impulse to stand up and scream. The caress became more insistent, and she found herself captivated by the strong hand gently stroking the nape of her neck. She lay absolutely still and dared not move even when the man laid himself full length next to her and took her in his arms. She felt like crying.

Later, the man wiped her tears away and got up. In her body, Lorraine felt an intense warmth and an absentminded and abstract confusion. She had liked him.

In her diary, Myra wrote:

A thousand cups and a million theories aren't worth a single week without Lorraine. I fooled myself completely with

*the chalice. I don't give a fuck about it. It is her warmth
and her love that are the real mystery.*

"Myra," I said when she closed her book, "Maria
wants to know if we would like to go out tonight.
We've been sulking for a week."

"No. I will stay home and read. You can go if you
want."

Maria and I went to Il Club, the place where we
had originally met. The whole gang was there, and
we spent a pleasant evening talking and trying not to
think of the matter that weighed so much on our
minds.

"Tomorrow is Friday," Lars reminded me when
we said our good-byes.

As if I didn't know. I was looking hopefully
toward tomorrow both because it was the beginning
of a long, arduous road toward recovering our lover
and because I was dying to find out what the monster kidnappers had in mind.

Myra was asleep when we returned. The book
was at her feet, and the light was still on. Maria
kissed me good night and went to her own quarters.

I studied Myra for a while. I loved her very much.
In her sleep she looked like a schoolgirl, Lorraine's
age; there was no suggestion of the brilliant scientist
and mature woman I had come to know. It was funny
watching her. At times she slept like a tigress, alert
and self-possessed as that time in Paris (it seemed so
long ago!) when I made love to her half-asleep. At
other times, like now, she seemed so vulnerable.

I disrobed and reached out to turn off the light, but
my arm stopped in midair. On the dresser were some
open telegrams. WE ARE FRANTIC Lorraine's father had

wired. WHERE ARE YOU, DAUGHTER? CALL US COLLECT The
telegram bore the address of our Paris hotel. Next to it
was another, from Professor Kaminsky: THERE WAS A
MAN HERE FROM THE FRENCH POLICE. HE WANTED TO KNOW
ABOUT YOUR LEGITIMACY. I REASSURED HIM. This too was
addressed to our Paris hotel, even though I remembered distinctly that Myra had written her husband
several times since we had moved into Maria Leone's,
keeping him *au courant* of the latest developments.

Most curious. On the dresser also was an edition
of the London Observer, and in an instant I identified
who must have been the reader of that venerable
newspaper: Signor Giacomo. He had been here,
bringing the mail.

I looked at Myra again, and this time I thought I
noticed, in her complete relaxation, another reason
for such blissful sleep.

It was very early. Myra was already up, applying
some makeup in the mirror.

I propped my head on my arms and looked at her.
"Was Giacomo here last night?"

"Yes, he brought some telegrams. It's Friday
today."

"I know. Why does your husband still write at the
Paris address?"

"It is an old telegram. It arrived when we were
leaving."

There was a rain shower on our way to Cinecittà, but
when we got out of the limousine it had stopped. There
were fewer people on the set than usual. Lars had sent
most of them away for the day, leaving only one camera crew of three men, Victor Borsa and himself.

"It's business as usual," he said. "These are the instructions. But we will film little until our new star shows up."

We waited in Lars's office, watching through the window as Maria Leone, Borsa and Lars rehearsed several scenes. I was having martinis for breakfast to calm myself. Myra had cigarette after cigarette.

At noon, we all had lunch together. There was no telephone call, no sign of anyone.

"If she is not here by five we are all going home," said Lars. "Business as usual stops at five."

I was becoming afraid. What if the terrorists had changed their mind? What if Lorraine was already dead? Perhaps she had tried to escape and *blam!* I tried not to verbalize any of this, but I knew Myra was panicking along the same lines.

"The ad was very clear," I reassured everyone. "We accepted their conditions completely. They responded. There is nothing to worry about."

Still, I felt queasy.

"Get some more coffee," Lars told his secretary on the on the intercom. We had finished our sandwiches.

"Time," said Maria, looking at her watch.

"Paolo, wait here a little longer," Myra asked.

"We must begin," Paolo said. "It has to be business as usual."

"Here is you coffee, sir!" Standing in the doorway holding a tray of coffee cups with a fresh, steaming pot of coffee was a pretty young woman in a flower-print dress.

"Who are you? I told my secretary no...."

"My name is Flora." She put the tray down on the desk and smiled.

ELEVEN

Flora was not alone. Shortly after she introduced herself, a young man appeared from behind the door.

"I am your production assistant," he said to Lars.

Maria Leone let out a subdued howl of indignation. "Carlo! You have the nerve!"

He gave her a steely gaze. "I do."

"We must begin work immediately," said Flora. "Where is the script?" Paolo handed them both copies of the script.

"How is she?" asked Myra.

"She is learning," said Carlo.

"Is she alive?" I asked.

"We are not killers. We are revolutionaries. This is from Lorraine." Flora took a tape out of her handbag. "Now you must go. We have work to do. Only people connected with the picture are allowed on the set."

This is what Lorraine said on the tape we heard when we got to Maria Leone's:

Hi, loves! I have been doing a lot of thinking. Many things they have told me make sense. I am well taken care of, and I have relative freedom of movement. It is very beautiful here, and there is a stream nearby. Sort of like summer camp. I miss both of you very much.... I want to be with you.

"I wonder if this couldn't be arranged," said Myra, after we listened to the tape a few times.

"What?"

"Being with her ... After all, they would have a better hand if they had another one of us...."

"You're nuts!"

"Let's try, Brandon.... I want to be with her. The child needs me."

The possibility that one of us might be able to join Lorraine in captivity was certainly very remote. If we asked, the terrorists might suspect some kind of plot and we might blow the whole thing. But I couldn't help dreaming about it. I almost forgot that it was Myra who wanted to join Lorraine. I saw myself doing it.

"I want to go...." I said.

No!" shouted Myra. "I *have* to go...."

Myra and I slugged it out all night. It was, of course, a hopeless, childish fantasy, but our fight made it almost real. Obviously, should it have been possible, we both wanted to go, but I was sure I was the best choice. There was, in Myra's eagerness, a certain guilt and a need to expiate for her imaginary maltreatment of Lorraine in Paris, and I didn't like that. It was almost dawn, and neither one of us had yet given in. We decided to solve the problem in the most impartial way. The shiny fifty-lire Italian coin flipped through the air three times, and the head it showed us settled the argument definitively by choosing me.

I cheated. Myra had no way of knowing that, since third grade, I'd been a champion coin-tosser. It was all so absurd!

But next day we gave it a try. I went to the set and asked Flora to give me a minute.

At first, she refused. I begged her.

"This, Mr. Stone, is the last time I am going to speak with you. You have exactly one minute."

"I would like very much to convince you of our innocence. We are not CIA agents. I am a writer, Dr. Kaminski is a professor and Lorraine...."

"We know what we need to know!"

"The thing is we love Lorraine...."

"Another bourgeois cliché!"

"I would hope you would stop interrupting me.... What I want is to join Lorraine in captivity. I am offering myself to you as a hostage in order to be with her."

I looked her straight in the eyes. She was unmoved. There was a contemptuous leer on her face. "I will submit your request to the YFA Command. Now I must be on the set."

It had been discouraging.

Later that evening, Paolo Lars wrung his hands in despair when we saw each other at Maria's. "It is horrifying!" he said. "They have changed the entire script.... It's vile! I can't direct such an atrocity. I

should have hired a director as I intended originally.... I cannot deal with these people! I am not a
Fascist monster, but there is a limit.... Do you know
what they have substituted for the beginning of the
picture?"

"The classroom scene?"

"Yes, it is now a laboratory of chemical warfare.
Generals and scientists sit around it discussing how
to eliminate enemies through sterilization.... It is dis-
gusting!"

"How is Flora?" asked Myra.

"She is not an actress," said Paolo, "but that
doesn't matter. We can dub her lines. She moves
gracefully enough."

"I hate her," said Maria, "but she is rather beautiful, no?" A dreamy expression crept into her counte-
nance.

"Maria! How can you?" Lars was indignant.

"Oh, it's nothing like that!" protested the actress.
"She insulted me six times today.... She called me a
bourgeois pig...."

"Wouldn't you know it?" said Lars. "Maria, *per
sangre di Dio*, it was you who brought Carlo here in
the first place! Have you no shame?"

That was rude. He didn't need to remind her.
Maria felt very bad about it. She constantly blamed
herself. She began to cry. At this point, the maid
announced Signor Giacomo. Before she was finished,
he was in the room.

"The terrorists live in the Penzione Estrella, near
the Central Train Station. They have a bare room with
a few books in it. After the filming is finished they go
there and stay. They have not been in communication
with anybody." He sat down.

Flora's departure caught Lorraine by surprise. She wasn't sorry to see Carlo go, but she felt that Flora had been kind to her. Two days had passed, and she had not been able to identify with any certainty the man who had made love to her in the night. During her "reeducation" classes, which continued uninterrupted, she looked thoughtfully at the faces in front of her. Silvio's hands, folded calmly in front of him were strong and masculine, but his eyes betrayed no knowledge of her body, no intimacy. Che had small, nervous hands and a skinny, tall body. It couldn't have been him. Curtis had a vigorous young body, wore tight pants and a T-shirt and his hands were also firm and calm. Neither one betrayed the slightest affection for her.

Lorraine worked every day alongside the men, cutting wood for the fire, cooking and washing clothes. There was a scrupulous distribution of work, and everyone's duties for the day were posted on the wall. At night she stayed awake, wondering if her secret lover would return. But two more nights passed, and he did not. Short of thinking that she had hallucinated the whole incident, Lorraine began to assume that it had been Carlo. This wasn't impossible. Carlo was a handsome man with strong hands also. She wasn't certain of anything any longer.

The thought crossed her mind that she ought to run away. But looking at the extraordinary high peaks with snow on them surrounding their encampment, she doubted very much that she would get anywhere. The dirt road on which they had come was completely overgrown by weeds, there was no sign of anyone having been there for years.

Slowly Lorraine began to see herself doomed forever to this kind of life. Her natural joviality and her sense of humor were not much appreciated by the company, so she fell silent.

After a week or maybe longer (there was no calendar or watch) she noticed that their canned supplies were getting low. Every day, they had opened the tins of beans and conserved meat and eaten them with flour tortillas cooked over the wood stove.

She realized that it would be much safer to pretend that the lessons in guerrilla philosophy had some impact on her. She found herself absentmindedly asking questions. This was seen by her captors as a hopeful sign, and they began treating her with a lot more respect. Silvio began calling her "comrade."

She had all but given up hope that any of the present company had been in bed with her that night. She hoped that things in Rome were going well and that she would be released. She looked forward also to the arrival of a new supply of food. At least there would be a new face.

And then, unexpectedly, a most curious discussion took place during one of her "reeducation" lessons.

"It is time," Silvio said, "to teach you how to have an orgasm. An unselfish, Communist orgasm...."

Lorraine looked at him, surprised like a nine-year-old hearing for the first time where babies come from. "I've had plenty of them," she said when she had recovered from shock.

"You have not," said Che.

"Outside," said Curtis.

Puzzled and intrigued, Lorraine rose to her feet and followed Curtis outside with the other two behind her. It was a sunny day. They stopped in the little grassy clearing near the creek. There were thousands of small flowers in the tall grass.

The men took off their clothes. Lorraine couldn't but admire their well-formed young bodies. Che had dark hair all over his chest and body, and his unaroused and uncircumcised penis looked impressive to her even in its sleep. Curtis had short blond hair on his muscular legs, but his strong chest was smooth. Silvio looked the best to Lorraine. He had a boyish yet manly body that betrayed an expectation. His muscles rippled up and down when he took off his shorts.

They stood in a close circle around her, and she could fell their strong, masculine warmth. Not knowing what else to do, Lorraine undid her dress at the back (it was one of Flora's tattered leftovers) and let it slide down to her ankles. She was wearing no underwear, and her tight buttocks appeared at once. Then she unbuttoned the shirt and let it slide off her round shoulders, allowing her upward-pointing breasts to bound arrogantly into view.

Naked now, she could feel her blood rushing to her heart, and a pleasant chill coursed through her. Her breath came on quicker as the men, not touching her yet, held her in a close circle. Without looking, she knew that the men were becoming erect. The softest touch of her thigh warned her Silvio's had come fully awake.

Some time passed during which no one moved. Lorraine could feel her desire growing, and she began to bite her lip to keep from lying down and spreading her legs wide. She felt she was all wet down there, and her pubic hair began to glisten. Her nipples were extraordinarily erect.

As if on a prearranged signal, the men came closer and touched her thighs and her left buttock with their erections. She felt the heads of their members on her skin, and when a drop of sperm wet her thigh she almost shouted. She didn't think she could stand it much longer. Every opening in her body felt relaxed, hospitable and wet. Involuntarily she ran her tongue over her lips, which felt chapped.

Lorraine leaned back into Curtis. He took her in his arms from behind and lowered her onto the grass on her back. She opened her legs wide, looking up at Che and Silvio. She saw there wasn't a single cloud in the sky. It was a warm blue day. But even though she was looking at the sky she could not help seeing, across it, the two thick masculinities of the men above her.

"Now," said Silvio, "you understand that this is your first free orgasm in the service of the people!"

Lorraine could care less what kind of orgasm this was going to be. All she wanted to do was draw the men into her, regardless. But she agreed, weakly nodding her head. Silvio lowered himself slowly between her outstretched legs. As he was entering her, Lorraine, who didn't want to scream, raised herself and took Che's in her mouth. One of her hands circled wildly in the air until it fastened on what it was looking for.

And thus, after some movement in which the sky went black several times, Lorraine had her first "people's orgasm," a series of them, actually. Maybe fifteen altogether.

Seated in the comfortable leather chair in Paolo Lars's office, Flora looked small for some reason. I was facing her, standing. She offered me a seat.

"I called you to inform you of the decision of the YFA command. After a great deal of deliberation it was decided that you will be allowed to join Lorraine in captivity."

I was stunned. My fantasy had come true.

"Of course," she said, "if there is any foul play, we will kill you. And if anything happens to us here, we will kill Lorraine. Is that understood?"

I acquiesced.

"Now, there are several things I must ask you in connection with this movie."

"Please."

"What is the social responsibility of a writer in the United States of America?"

I didn't quite understand. "I write about people.... I am responsible to my characters, to my work...."

"You are not answering me. Let's take this scene. You are in your hotel room in Paris, writing. Lorraine approaches you and accuses you of not serving the people through your writing...."

The absurdity of such a situation brought an unwarranted smile to my lips. Flora looked at me severely.

"Well ... I would probably say to her: 'What people?' I don't know...."

"And then she would say to you: 'You are a reactionary. The revolution needs strong creators to prepare society for the future.'"

By no stretch of imagination did I see Lorraine saying such a thing. But I let it ride. "She might...."

Flora made some notes, then dismissed me. "Your instructions will arrive in the mail," she said.

"Thank you."

Walking out of there, I felt apprehensive. But the

thought of rejoining Lorraine made me immensely happy. I felt terrible about Myra though.

"It is absolutely impossible!" said Signor Giacomo. "They have not left their room at the *pensione* a single time during the past five days without a tail. They did not visit anybody, they did not speak to anybody. I have run checks on all the merchants they came in contact with. They have their dinners at the *pensione*, and every guest was thoroughly scrutinized by our agency."

"Nevertheless, they must have communicated with their command somehow," I said.

"Hmmm." Signor Giacomo looked very thoughtful. "Suppose there is no YFA command, suppose the two here and the two or three who are holding Lorraine are the whole outfit."

"My dear Giacomo," Lars said impatiently, "the YFA has been active for a long time. You know as much as there is to know about them. They are a well-known group."

"What are they known for?" asked Giacomo. "A number of daring robberies, an endless stream of manifestos and this kidnapping. The bombings attributed to them have not been confirmed; they could be anybody's work."

"What are you trying to say?" asked Myra.

"Nothing … I am speculating."

The instructions came typed in a letter addressed to me, c/o Maria Leone, at the studio. According to this I was to buy a one-way ticket on the Orient Express, Rome–Bucharest. I should take a seat in compartment number six at the front of the train. At one of the stations during the two-days-and-one-night ride I would be approached by someone.

"Ah, now we can begin to study the map," said Giacomo.

We bent over the atlas.

"The Orient Express makes forty-two stops along the route." Giacomo ran his finger across a number of countries. "Austria, Hungary, Rumania. Two of these are Communist countries, and this brings up an interesting question. Is either Hungary or Rumania a terrorist haven? Officially, I am sure they would deny such a charge. But is it possible?"

Alonso, who was also present as a legal witness to the proceedings, said: "I don't think Rumania.... They've been going out of their way to improve their image in the West. They are seeking trade agreements. Hungary has also, recently, opened up to the West and is cultivating a pro-European policy...."

That would leave Austria.... Highly unlikely...."

"Precisely, Giacomo."

"Look.... Whatever you may deduce, I do not want *anybody*, and I mean that emphatically, to interfere with my journey. They said they would kill me, and they will if there is even a shadow of suspicion!"

I had a sudden, unpleasant vision of Flora's cold gaze as she emptied the contents of a revolver into my head. It was a definite possibility. I shuddered. I was a long way from the San Francisco school system. Or was it all that long? There had been, among my students in those remote days, quite a number of angry rebels. I had always sympathized with them, knowing their home conditions, their restlessness. But I had never imagined them brandishing guns and kidnapping. Now I could see the possibility.

Giacomo interrupted my reverie. "You can rest assured there will be nothing to endanger your lives. I promise."

Myra cried. My train was leaving the very next day. This would be the last night we would share a bed. I touched her shoulder lightly with my palm. She let herself collapse against me.

Giacomo, Alonso and Creghi, who was also there being very taciturn and unlike his ebullient self, wished me luck. These men were my friends, I realized, as I shook their hands warmly.

Maria was out for the evening. We were alone, Myra and I. An array of images of our life together flashed through my mind. Our fateful meeting as I took the wrong turn to the kitchen. Our passion in the small room of Lorraine's dormitory. The balcony in Naples. The breakfasts in Paris. Image upon image. When and if I would write my book I would dedicate many loving pages to this woman. I stroked her hair and kissed her cheeks.

The train chugged seductively in the endless night of the Hungarian steppes, imposing its rhythm on my tense mind, over the sleepless days and nights. I slept in fits and starts. At every border, I was rudely awakened by customs officials who got ruder and more brutal the farther we got. Everything appeared to me in a haze, and the world was slightly underwater. Through my red eyelids I watched the procession of human formalities with the resigned detachment of a dreamer.

I was going to join Lorraine. As I had done often during this endless ride, I brought her to my mind. Lorraine zipping up her leather jacket in an expensive restaurant while the horrified maitre d' stood by stiffly; Lorraine's legs spread apart on satin sheets; Lorraine with her mouth poised in an absolute impish O; Lorraine walking on the street; sleeping; swimming; Lorraine standing thoughtfully, leaning against a tree; the Lorraine of the book I was going to write; the Lorraine of Myra's diary.

Myra tried to shake away the feeling of dread she was experiencing. Just now she had filled six pages of her diary with stupid recriminations. It was not her fault. But she felt both alone and responsible, a position that left her weak and afraid. She tried to gather herself together. In our absence, she would quietly do research, try to find out more about the chalice, occupy her time to the hilt. Having made this decision, she felt a little better. She made an appointment with Father Benedetti at the Vatican. She also resolved to avoid sexual encounters for a time. She wanted to be alone with her research. Besides, the last night with Brandon was fantastic, she told herself. She woke up with a lightness in her body. Their lovemaking had had a tragic urgency because of the separation. It had been better than ever.

True, it had been a memorable night. But it hadn't been just Myra, and this perhaps is one of the reasons why I felt so tired and so eerie. After Myra had fallen asleep around four in the morning, I went into the main living room to smoke a cigarette. I couldn't sleep. I had on a short Chinese gown with a dragon on the back. I was sitting in a chair looking at the extinct fireplace, pondering my departure the next day, when Maria Leone came in.

"You must give Lorraine something from me," she said.

She was wearing a gown similar to the one she had worn the first night we stayed in her house, a filmy affair that hid nothing.

She pulled my rather reluctant person by the hand to a room at the end of the hallway. I followed her in. In the dim reddish light I saw that the room consisted entirely of a baldachin bed with blue satin covers on it. I had not seen this room in our entire stay here. With a hurried gesture, Maria pushed her gown over her head and looked at me, stark naked. I was rather taken aback, though certainly not by her flawless body with its wide black patch and its full, firm breasts over which her long black hair cascaded.

"It's for Lorraine," she said. "I have not made love to a man for five years. You must take my love to her."

Maria came very close, then fell on her knees and undid the gold cord that held my gown together. She licked my already overexerted phallus with a slow, dreamy stroke. I became aroused. I lifted her gently and put her on the satin spread. She opened her legs wide and, with her hand, she brought me into her, moaning a little with panic and excitement.

It was a short, sweet experience, and when I returned to the bedroom Myra was awake. She guessed at once.

"I'm sure Lorraine will love the gift," she said without the slightest trace of jealousy.

"Take care, Brandon!"

"Take care, love!"

I was worried about Myra. I hoped she would soon recover her cool self and continue her research as the drama unfolded, but I knew she would have a hard time.

My thoughts unfocused again, and the endless train tracks outside the window began their monotonous rhythm again. I was alone in compartment number six at the front of the train. Judging from the monotony of the landscape, we were still in Hungary. Occasionally little lights flickered by with the late-night desperation of small villages lost in the vastness of the *pusta*.

Soon I would cross the last border into Rumania, the last country at the end of this ride which began in the civilized comfort of Rome and might end in God-knows-what backward place of tribal ritual.

I was falling again into one of my light trances when the door of the compartment opened and a man whose face I could not see in the dark walked in. He sat on the seat opposite from me. I felt him studying me intently in the obscurity.

"I hope you are comfortable. Please have a Turkish cigarette," he said. Those were the code words.

TWELVE

Suddenly, the train made an unscheduled stop. The man facing me pulled the emergency switch over the window. The express came to a screeching halt.

"Let's go" he said. Firmly, he grasped my shoulder and led me to the darkened corridorand from there to the door. We walked out into the rather cold night, which made me suspect we were in the mountains.

A car pulled up alongside the train, and we got in the back. The driver wore a ski mask. He made a sharp turn, and we began driving straight up, it seemed, on a narrow road full of hairpin turns and twists. I pored over the map I had studied. We were somewhere one hundred to two hundred kilometers east of the Hungarian border, which would just about place us in Transylvania. I tried to keep track of the turns in the road, but I soon lost count.

"Out," said the mask. It was almost dawn; bluish light seeped in from afar. "Spread against the car."

In classic police style he searched me briskly, taking away my wallet, my lighter and my pen.

"From here we walk."

The road had ended, turning into a donkey path. The view was impressive: nothing but straight rock rising vertically over green and blue belts. The path was merely a narrow illusion between treacherous drops, boulders and pines.

We must have been walking for two hours when it suddenly came into view. "It" was a magnificent fortified castle built no doubt sometime in the sixteenth century. It stood like a fairy tale vision, completely solitary, its towers piercing the clouds, an unnatural silence surrounding it.

I secretly congratulated myself for the whim which, a few years back, had had me studying medieval fortifications. I have often noticed how the most apparently useless bits of knowledge come in handy at unexpected times. I knew almost instinctively the layout of the place, and although I had not seen this particular one anyplace, I knew it to be similar to the other hundreds of sixteenth-century fortresses in Transylvania. Transylvania had been, throughout the Middle Ages, the refuge of fierce nobles who had quarreled with their king. In the impenetrable desolation of these mountains they had built themselves powerful abodes.

We stopped to breathe. My two guards kept a morose silence.

"Is that where she is?" I asked, pointing at the castle.

They didn't answer. We resumed our climb. We were scaling an embankment, sliding on pine needles. I was the first to reach the edge of the rock on which the vast foundation of the castle stood. Now is my chance, I thought. The man on the train was pulling himself up on the rock. A gun stuck out of his back pocket. I was about to bend over and take the gun and then push him over with my foot. But the ski mask, who was only a few paces behind, looked up and, in a flash, he pointed a revolver at me. I hadn't even moved.

"I wasn't doing anything," I protested.

He shook his head but kept the gun in his hand.

I had been forbidden to wear a watch, but I would say it was about nine in the morning. From the rock I had a wide view of the mountains glistening with their snowy peaks around us. I was almost sure the depression between the two tallest mountains was Bran Pass. I knew where we were. Ironically, not far from here was the residence of the legendary Dracula. I had always wanted to go and visit one day.

A small gate let us through into an ancient courtyard. The courtyard was protected from view by strong walls. There were a number of holes going in. I imagined them to be doors.

The masked man took off the ski mask, shoved his gun in my back and said: "Walk very slowly."

I did. We were in a narrow, dark passage. The walls were wet and felt slimy to the touch. I carefully stepped down the slippery stairs.

"Wait!"

I stopped. I had the eerie feeling that there was no one else in the place. "Is Lorraine here?" I asked.

Without answering, the man from the train unbolted what seemed like a dungeon door and pushed me through. I fell onto my face on a stone floor, hitting my head. I heard the door being bolted behind. I was alone.

When Lorraine returned from the creek where she had been washing clothes with Che standing guard, she had a shock. The previously empty food shelf was full of cans and sacks of beans, flour and rice. Silvio was sitting at the table reading.

"Who brought the food?" she said.

"The tooth fairy," replied Silvio without taking his eyes off the book. Lorraine couldn't believe her eyes. She still couldn't, later that evening, when she saw that there were still only four of them. She tried to broach the subject again but was met with rebuff.

She stood awake, thinking. She had noticed, several times, one or the other of the men leaving the encampment for almost a whole day. She had assumed that they went walking in the woods to think or practice shooting. She often heard what seemed like distant shots. There was another target range near the shack, where they had been teaching her to use a machine gun. This was actually a log with a number of rocks on it. They were becoming so convinced of Lorraine's "conversion" that they had started training her. They had also become rather careless with their weapons, and Lorraine could have seized a number of opportunities to try something desperate. But she waited instead; she felt that it would be futile.

Since the time when they had taught her about the "people's orgasm," the guerrillas had again displayed a singular lack of interest in her charms. Lorraine was baffled. She had been very mad at herself after that experience for not being able to control her emotions. In spite of what her physical being told her, she couldn't help hating her captors. It was wrong, she felt, to submit. She resolved to fight them off next time. But there was no next time. It was most curious.

Now that she thought of it, she also realized that whenever they left for a long time, they returned looking extremely satisfied, almost as if ... yes, almost as if they had been well fucked.

I must, I must! Lorraine kept thinking, watching the guerrillas sleep. It was very light in the shack; the moon was full.

Shivering lightly, Lorraine got up on her tiptoes. She walked over the body of Silvio, who stirred vaguely in his sleep. She made for the door but then remembered the guns. The guerrillas liked to hang their guns and cartridge belts on a number of hooks around Mao's portrait. She took down a machine gun and a belt. Pointing it vaguely at the bodies sleeping on the floor, she tried to imagine pulling the trigger. It would have been easy, but she couldn't do it. They are kids, she thought, just like me.

Outside it was even colder. She gritted her teeth. She slung the gun over her left shoulder and fastened the belt across her chest. She started walking into the direction the men took during their disappearances.

For some time it did not feel very difficult, pushing through the woods. There was no path. Soon, the forest bed began a steep climb.

Lorraine sat on a rock contemplating the climb. What in the world could be up there? Barely a few feet from her a silvery snake was crawling toward

God-knows-what hole. Lorraine gave a start, but the snake looked unconcerned.

"Friend, can you tell me which way? You must know these parts pretty well."

The snake just kept going, and then suddenly he disappeared under a rock. Lorraine shook her head looking at him, then noticed the rock he had gone under. It wasn't just any rock. It was a slab of stone, a perfectly square slab.

She pushed it with her foot, and it moved a bit. Falling to her knees, she threw her whole weight against it. The stone slid without any difficulty, revealing under it a series of steps going straight down. Cautiously, she went in.

Father Benedetti was happy to see Dr. Myra Kaminski.

"Madame, you have occasioned me a great deal of thought since you were last here."

He bade her sit. Father Benedetti's office was a mess of books and manuscripts. From the walls of the paneled room hung a number of portraits of former fathers of the Church.

Myra sat on the leather chair.

Standing up, the father continued: "I became intrigued once more by the mystery of the Lorraine cup. Although the Church does not like to be reminded of it, the...."

"The *what*, Father?" said Myra.

"Oh, I'm sorry, madame. What is it you want to know?"

"The *Lorraine* cup ... I thought the miracle happened in Loire...."

"It did. But the cup, as you undoubtedly know,

was last seen in Lorraine at the end of the war.... You know, Alsace and Lorraine?"

I did not know. Neither Monsieur Jerome nor Captain LaCrosse even mentioned the fact.... On the contrary, they pointed out Loire as the sole location.... I have a list from Captain LaCrosse of the witnesses to the miracle ... who are all dead, by the way."

"Ah. That is strange indeed. The cup was taken to Lorraine, according to our documents, by a group of Resistance fighters.... Many died there, and the cup disappeared...."

"Monsieur LaCrosse's group, by any chance?"

"As a matter of fact, yes."

"We were purposely misled...."

"It would appear that way. In light of this, I am beginning to see other things. As you know, the miracle was accepted officially by the Church. The wartime misery of the faithful may have had something to do with the official acceptance of the miracle. In normal times there would have been the long process of proving it beyond any shadow of doubt. As it was, the acceptance was based mainly on Father Bourget's report and Monsieur's ratification...."

"But Monsieur Jerome died...."

"Indeed."

"How many miracles has the Church officially certified in the past thirty years?"

"That is exactly the point, madame. In our *entire* century there have been only seven certified miracles ... and in each of these cases a central piece of evidence is missing. The Loire Cup, or the Lorraine cup as you prefer, is only the last in a line."

"When we were here last time you did not know

that the cup of Persephone and the Loire cup were the same object...."

"We still do not know. But allow me to continue. From Lourdes, the second icon of the Virgin is missing, from Valencia the Jesus Rising is missing ... a big statue, too...."

"That is astonishing. None of this seems to be publicly known."

"The Church prefers it that way."

"But is there no active investigation?"

"At the urging of the French Church, the last investigation was ended in 1952.... The cases are open, but there is no budget...."

Myra had a hard time absorbing all of this. "My circumstances at the moment do not permit me to continue searching ... but I expect you to do something. I would be extremely grateful if you kept me informed."

"At this point, madame, I must be very discreet. But I promise you I will be at your service when you need me. I would be grateful also if you would maintain silence on the subject ... and on our conversation. Public outcry might hurt."

"I understand perfectly."

In her diary that afternoon, Myra scrawled, in excited handwriting, the extraordinary revelation:

It cannot simply be coincidence! THE LORRAINE CUP! If it is coincidence, it is an accident of the, highest order. My sweet Lorraine!

A little later, the scientist surfaced:

Of course it is a coincidence. There is no end to this kind of absurdity. Next thing you know the cup will be hidden in a quiche Lorraine…. Oh God!

Lorraine felt her way into the darkness, cursing herself for not taking the flashlight. The gun felt heavy on her shoulder, and she began to sweat. The leather gun belt was sliding up and down her shirt. She nearly fell into a trap. Her foot, poised for the next step, felt nothing there. She squatted and felt around with her hands. There was nothing there either. It must have been a collapsed portion of the stairway. She sat on the step and thrust her feet into the dark. She felt water on her toes. Lorraine lowered herself into a murky pool that came up to her waist. Holding her gun over her head, she walked cautiously through it. Stories of ancient horrors in ancient tunnels came to her mind. She remembered reading a story once about nests of vipers that lived in musty underground passages. Of traps set for the stranger inside old stairs. She was afraid. Just as she was about to turn around, she felt another step.

The tunnel came to an abrupt end a few hundred feet later at a massive wooden door locked by enormous barnacled iron locks. With her hands, Lorraine explored the door. The locks were indeed enormous, but it wasn't them holding the door in place. They were rusted and useless, hanging from broken hinges. The real fastener was a steel bolt, shiny and smooth to the touch. She pulled it.

It was completely dark inside. With both her hands thrust in front of her, Lorraine took a step forward. Someone grabbed her from behind and put a hand over her mouth. She fainted.

"When did you know it was me?"

"When I felt your tits."

"Liar!"

She rested her head in my lap. I caressed her hair, thinking. There were still a few hours before dawn when, undoubtedly, the guerrillas would notice Lorraine's disappearance and head straight for the secret passage. But we stood an excellent chance of escaping.

"I missed you, love."

"I missed you."

"Poor Myra's been hating herself ever since Paris. She thinks it's been her fault."

"Oh, Myra," said Lorraine, "I love you; don't think that."

"Perhaps we'll have a chance to tell her that ourselves. Where is the shack?"

"Less than a mile from here."

"You never saw the castle from that side?"

"Never."

"That's incredible. From what I know about castles in this area, there are only three that would be so well protected.... Bran ... and this isn't Bran because I've seen pictures of it, and the two Hunyadi castles.... It must be one of those...."

"Who's that?"

"Hunyadi was a Hungarian count who was banished from court and spent the rest of his life fortifying his castles and...." I fell silent.

"And what?"

"Well, there were rumors during his lifetime that he was into human sacrifices, black masses, that kind of stuff.... He was also quite an art collector.... He was the lover of the empress for a while, and she gave him half the Vienna gallery for a present...."

"This dingy joint?"

"These are the dungeons, love. It must be something else upstairs. I thought all these places were museums.... It's strange."

"Do you think they're holding us in the basement of a museum?"

"No.... You've seen one road and I've seen the other.... The place is inaccessible. They've probably carted the stuff to the capital."

"What do we do?"

"Get out and try to steal the car."

"Brandon...."

"Yes, love?"

"Would you make love to me?"

You could count on Lorraine for incongruity. This was certainly the Lorraine I knew. We were two shivering creatures in a putrid dungeon in danger of being killed, and Lorraine wanted....

Before I had formulated the whole thought she had pulled my pants down and fastened her lips to my cock.

"For Chrissakes...."

She undid the fatigue pants she was wearing and slid her firm, full buttocks square onto my erection.

Well, it was too late for protest, so I slipped inside her and began to fuck. It was a short, sweet affair full of all the yearning for each other we had carried for this long.

We both came swiftly, convulsively.

I buttoned up my pants, helped Lorraine with the safety pin that held her outfit together and slung the machine gun over my shoulder.

We went into the tunnel and started to make our way back outside. I had seen enough plans of underground passages from medieval forts to know that they led to more than one place. And surely, when we traced our steps back to the water hole where Lorraine had nearly fallen, I felt a pretty narrow opening to the left.

"Hold my hand. I'm going in...."

Holding Lorraine's hand, I pushed myself in sideways. The ground was solid. "Come."

Lorraine was in, and we pushed forward.

"Myra, you are so unhappy. Is there anything I can do for you?" Maria motioned the maid to leave the room.

"There is so much," Myra said. "Everything is completely mysterious. I don't know what any of this is all about...."

"I know, darling. My life on the set has become a nightmare. Carlo and Flora run the movie like an armed camp.... We can't go anywhere during the breaks.... I have had to play so many stupid scenes.... It is incredible...."

Myra was sympathetic. "I know...."

Later that evening, Maria went out. Myra had refused, as she had done a number of times. The maid was also out. She sat alone, thinking. The house was very quiet. A window was open, and smells from the garden filed the air with a floral sweetness.

Myra was startled to see Signor Giacomo standing there.

"How did you get in?"

"Very quietly. Get a suitcase, put some clothes in it and follow me."

"What's going on?"

"I'll explain later. Do as I say."

A few minutes later, Signor Giacomo helped Myra out the open window. From there they walked through the garden and used a side entrance to reach the street. Giacomo's Mercedes was parked there.

"What will Maria think?"

"You can call her later. There are several developments. I know where they are holding Lorraine and Brandon. We must go to Bucharest and register an official protest with the government."

Giacomo explained the situation. From his slightly tired looks Myra deduced immediately that he must have been on the road for days.

The tunnel came to another abrupt end in front of a massive door. On this one, rusted old locks testified to the fact that no one had been here since at least the seventeenth century. I pulled most of them off with my hand. A thousand dead spider empires fell in a cloud of dust as I labored. Behind the door was some kind of giant piece of furniture. Lorraine and I put our collective shoulders to it and pushed. It did not budge. It was discouraging.

"We should go the way I came," said Lorraine.

Just then I realized that the thing, whatever it was, stood on some legs and there was room underneath to crawl through. We did. It felt very still and very soft inside. We listened for human sounds. There were none. Walking about, I hit a table with my hip and almost screamed. On the table, however, was a candleholder. Lorraine fumbled for matches and lit the candle inside.

Crystal chandeliers; vases; gnarled, carved griffins and paintings burst suddenly around us. It was a long, narrow room with a painted ceiling on which a gilded representation of Greek bacchanalia danced with shadows of nymphs, satyrs and cloud cherubs.

Lorraine whistled. The room was also full of small cases of Morocco-bound books. The reddish leather threw an eerie tint into the light. Fascinating titles such as *The Devil: A Study by a Longtime Confessor; His Habits, His Hiding Places, His Manifestions and His Jokes* (in Latin) drew my attention.

"Someone lives here," Lorraine said, pointing to a pair of silk panties draped over the marble head of a faun's bust.

There were other such touching signs. A pair of likewise silk stockings were draped over a Dutch landscape leaning against a wall. One often sees, when one sweeps the drive-in movie theaters of America in the early hours of dawn, underpants and stockings just like these hanging from microphone poles. A beautiful blue globe of Steuben glass was stuffed with garter belts.

A sensual and eclectic taste had put this room together. I pushed open a tall white door and yet another extraordinary room appeared.

"I found a light switch," said Lorraine. She flipped it on and, indeed, a reddish electric light poured from an abajoured lamp in a corner. The cherry light reflected off a number of stained-glass windows treating also of magnificent bacchanalia. But the main feature of the room was the extraordinary number of mirrors there. Long Venetian mirrors in oval frames projected a hundred Lorraines and Brandons around the room.

"Turn it off. Light a candle."

"I can't quite imagine guerrillas living here," said

Lorraine.

I quickly took hold of the gun and pointed it at the shadow that had appeared in a doorway.

"Cut it out, Derrain!" the shadow said in a sleepy female voice. "What are you doing here, anyway? This isn't your...."

When she saw she had made a mistake, the girl froze. I made her sit.

"Who else is here?"

The girl was French. "Oh, monsieur, I am so afraid.... "

"If you faint on me, I will kill you," I said, in my best Clint Eastwood voice.

"There are only the girls here...."

"How many?"

"Seven, monsieur. They are all sleeping in there." She pointed to the door she had come from.

"What is this, a dormitory?" asked Lorraine, bringing her candle closer to study the woman. She was stunningly beautiful.

"This is a ... harem, monsieur."

"Whose?"

"Oh, the cardinal's, of course."

Visions of Justine started dancing in front of my eyes. This was too bizarre.

"Who is this cardinal?"

"Oh, monsieur, he is a very important man."

"Who guards the harem?"

"Tonight it is Derrain and André."

When she had described Derrain and André to me, I realized that they were the men who had brought me here.

"Is there anyone else in the castle?"

At this point a strange feeling compelled me to turn

sharply and point my weapon at another shadow.

"Put your hands up, LaCrosse," said Lorraine, who had also turned.

THIRTEEN

This country, it seemed to Myra, who had been in Bucharest for forty-eight hours, was full of men and women who endlessly twisted unlit cigarettes between their fingers. The reason, perhaps, was the modern age, which had taken away people's rosary beads and replaced them with cigarettes. But it would have been in extremely bad taste to mention anything too religious to the bald man who appraised her severely in the spacious office thirty stories above the street.

This building, blessed by a narrow-minded architect with a kind of grim efficiency, was Kafkaesque. They had been shuffled in a bizarre order through a succession of white rooms, dominated by the stern gazes of Marx, Lenin and Ceausescu. An extra-large mural of *Aviation Workers Smiling at the Future* ran the whole length of the hallway. Finally, after futile hours of bureaucratic impediments, Signor Giacomo and Myra were taken to what they were made to understand was the head man.

Colonel Lammai of the Party Security Division stood like a bald adverb in the middle of the monochromatic sentence around them. He was squat, dark and immensely muscular, and the position of his lips suggested that he had never smiled.

"I understand you have an important matter to discuss."

Signor Giacomo looked straight into his narrow pupils. "It is my understanding that you will take this matter directly to your premier."

"If it is a serious matter."

"We have sufficient evidence that your country is sheltering a terrorist group. This evidence, needless to say, could prove extremely embarrassing...."

When Giacomo dropped the name of Captain Jean-Pierre LaCrosse, Colonel Lammai stood up sharply. He rummaged through his desk for a Havana cigar, which he stuck into his mouth without lighting.

"I will convey your information," he said. They were dismissed.

It was the best hotel in Bucharest, or so they had been told. It was a twenty-story box that gave onto a main square. This square was dominated by a square cement box with a limp red flag atop. Surrounding the two monoliths, however, were pleasant clusters of Byzantine, Viennese, Greek, French colonial and Turkish houses swathed here and there by tree-lined boulevards. In the distance, faint clumps of glass-and-cement towers rose in the drizzly rain.

Myra gazed out the window at an unnaturally

large portrait of Ceausescu overlooking the square. Evening fell, and the man's figure lit up, suddenly sending pudgy little bags of bureaucratic fat careening through the air.

"This place gives me the creeps," said Myra.

"It is our only chance. I believe the Rumanians cannot afford the scandal. They will pretend the guerrillas have crossed into the country illegally, and they will roust them out. I made it clear that the Italian press is set to go if they refuse."

"Yes, but what if they give the guerrillas advance warning? Then it's good-bye Lorraine and Brandon.... I'm so afraid...."

Giacomo caressed Myra's hair. "We hope for the best." Myra turned and let herself be held by Giacomo's bear strength. She opened her lips a little when he kissed her.

Colonel Lammai called promptly next morning. It was still drizzling outside.

They dressed, took the elevator down and hailed a taxi. They were in no mood for the taxi driver's jokes, but the man felt obliged to tell funny jokes at the expense of his country.

"There are two men, see, standing on the street watching a Cadillac. 'What a beautiful Pobeda!' says one. That's a Russian car. 'What's the matter with you?' asks the other. 'Can't you tell a Cadillac from a Pobeda? Don't you know a Cadillac when you see one?' 'I know a Cadillac,' says the one, 'but I don't know you!'"

Lammai was not alone. With him was the premier, looking exactly as if he had descended from the poster in front of the hotel.

"My government," he said, "will assist you in

every way possible. We will deploy a contingent to arrest the guerrillas this very afternoon. What are your conditions for keeping the affair secret?"

"We only want the safe release of our friends, Mr. Premier. That is all."

A little later, a black limousine swallowed Myra and Giacomo, and they were taken to an army post a few miles out of the city. There, eighteen armored cars filled with Rumanian soldiers stood ready to depart for the Carpathian Alps.

Although LaCrosse maintained a sullen silence, the girls had plenty to say. They were all awake and inside the room. With their help we had barricaded the room with statues and furniture, tables and lamps. There were still two or three hours before dawn. André and Derrain were also inside, disarmed.

"We did not know that, monsieur...." one of the girls, a beautiful melancholy looking teenager, said, in answer to my question about whether they had known that the "cardinal" was actually a captain of the French police.

"All we knew, monsieur, is that the cardinal demanded absolute obedience for the four months we were to spend here...."

"Absolute!" said a blond who looked like Monique.

"Are you all French?" asked Lorraine.

"No, mademoiselle. I am Belge."

"I am from Mozambique," a light-toned Negro girl said.

The girls came from everywhere. Apparently they had been lured by the extraordinary money and the romance of the place.

"Who recruited you?"

"Two French girls … Monique and Colline," answered the Belgian.

LaCrosse shook his head in dismay. He was wearing a black monk's robe similar to the one he had worn at Lorraine's "initiation." This was how she had instantly recognized him.

But Lorraine was intent on provoking as much dismay as possible in the hapless captain. "What did you have to do?"

The girls looked at each other, chuckling. "Come here, mademoiselle…." said the blond.

Lorraine went there. The pubescent youth pulled a gold string, revealing a window to another room. I glanced that way too.

In there marble satyrs plugged each other shamelessly in the ass and bare-bottomed rose marble beauties received finely veined marble fascias across their immortal cracks, while copper vases nearly collapsed from the orgiastic weight of the figures carved on their sides. Drinking bowls offered the lips of their bronze vaginas to the drinkers, pitchers offered their penile spouts to the porcelain vaginas of an array of cups. Goblets of intertwined gold lovers offered eager protrusions to the refined lips. Strewn in seeming disorder among these were a number of pensive male and female statues with their mosaic fingers curled or stuck in their wealth of shameless detail.

"What did you do in there?" I asked after I drew my breath from the extraordinary shock.

The Mozambique beauty, barely wearing anything except a frilly little silk chemise, looked at me mischievously. "You want to see?"

I did want to see, but I liked to feel safe. The room

was barricaded, and I had to keep my eyes on the three men. But Lorraine really did want to see. "What about them?"

"Let's tie them up."

With the gold cord of the various draperies we had enough rope to tie down an army. Lorraine, with aid from the girls, tied the three men to the chairs, from head to foot.

Mozambique pushed open the window to the other room (it was, apparently, the only way to get in) and began to demonstrate what for Monsieur LaCrosse must have been a breakfast treat.

Going straight toward a bronze Hercules aiming a bronze penis at us, she lowered herself gracefully on the erection of the statue, holding the ancient god by his neck with her hands. Expertly, she fucked him.

I had barely recovered from the strange sight when she dismounted and began, in rapid succession, to make love to all the objects ideally suited to a young girl's fantasies. Directly aroused marble fauns lying on their backs offered her their Carrara erections. Why, even the armrests of chairs and couches offered erectile bumps for the so inclined.

In spite of the obviously tense situation, I could feel electricity in the room. Lorraine was definitely impressed.

"Just think," she said, "all this time I was wondering why the guerrillas wouldn't touch me. Now I know why."

"Oh, mademoiselle, the boys from the camp never saw this room...."

"They must have seen something," Lorraine insisted. "They looked awfully satisfied when they came back from the castle."

"Oh, that is a whole different thing.... We had to dress up like them, in fatigues, when they came over...."

"They didn't know this was a harem?"

"Oh, no.... They thought this was the supreme command of their movement ... the 'cardinal's elite guard'.... We were instructed to teach them 'people's orgasms'...."

"That's incredible, LaCrosse.... I must hand it to you. You sold those kids on Maoist and Reichian claptrap while you were having a ball with the Marquis de Sade...."

"I did not sell them anything...." said LaCrosse. "This is all part of the revolutionary tactics of the movement."

"You're kidding," said Lorraine, reciting from her reeducation classes. "... in a world where men and women are perfectly equal there will be no slavery, prostitution and decadence...."

"That is so," said LaCrosse, "but we must work to achieve that world."

"The end justifies the means," I put in my ironic two-cents' worth, "especially when the means are the fantasies of Captain LaCrosse.... You are raving mad, monsieur...."

I don't know where our discussion might have led us if at this point I had not heard footsteps outside the room and someone trying to force the door to the secret passage.

"Silence!" I pointed the machine gun toward the entrance.

"Derrain, what is the matter? Why is it locked?" asked a voice.

Lorraine recognized Silvio.

"Silvio, this is Lorraine. Brandon is here, and we are holding LaCrosse, Derrain and André prisoners. We have a machine gun and two revolvers ..."

The guerrillas could be heard consulting.

"Lorraine," said Che, "we are going to storm through the door. We are giving you three minutes to reconsider. We have enough dynamite to take the whole place apart...."

"If you do," I said, "I am going to kill LaCrosse ... then Derrain ... then André ... and you are not going to come through without casualties!"

"There are seven girls here also, Che. Think of them."

"They are our comrades.... They will die like the rest of us."

"Comrades, my ass," said Lorraine. "They are LaCrosse's personal whores...."

"Liar."

"Tell him, girl!" Lorraine motioned to the French blond.

"I am afraid this is true, Che. We were told to lie. We are not revolutionaries.... We have been paid by LaCrosse...."

There were a few tense moments of silence.

"We must speak to LaCrosse.... LaCrosse, can you hear us?"

I took the gag out of his mouth. "Speak to your boys, LaCrosse!"

"It is a misunderstanding, Silvio!" LaCrosse said. "It is true they have been paid, but my revolutionary allegiance and dedication remain unchanged.... I must be allowed to explain!"

"You will explain a lot!" said Silvio. "Brandon!"

"I'm here!"

"We guarantee you safe passage out of here if you will deliver LaCrosse to us."

I looked at Lorraine. She shook her head.

"I'm afraid not, Silvio. As much as I would personally like to, I think he is entitled to a proper trial."

"Absolutely," said Lorraine.

LaCrosse looked relieved. It was the first time I ever remembered seeing a human expression on his face.

The guerrillas held another consultation.

"We are momentarily at a standstill!" said Curtis. "But we have taken a vote. We have decided to give you a full thirty minutes to change your minds. We are placing dynamite all around the place. In exactly thirty minutes we are going to leave. From the time we leave, you have exactly ten minutes before the explosion."

In the limousine, driving slowly behind the armored vehicles, Myra studied the landscape with a terrible sense of foreboding. She didn't trust the Communists, in spite of Giacomo's reassurances. What if all of this was a trap? What if, when they arrived, they were placed under arrest?

They passed through an industrial city. Smokestacks dotted the purplish sky. It must have been a chemical factory. It smelled vile. Like Poincaré said, once and for all times: "It's the scale that makes the phenomenon!" The size of things in this city seemed to exist in a shifting scale of ideological belligerence. The meanest fat men adorned the walls, the loudest tractor music climbed the walls where the radio was, the slowest red clouds drifted upward toward the Party Pantheon in the sky. The words of the slogans claiming the sides of buildings were blown to sizes way beyond anyone's humble sense of the vocabulary or of humor. Humor loves miniatures (as does Webster), but it is often at a loss with gigantism.

Her mind was wandering. Thinking of the Iron Curtain, another incongruous analogy offered itself to her. Years ago, when her first boyfriend Fred had collapsed after a frustrating attack on her virginity, he had exclaimed: "It's the Iron Curtain!" Myra smiled. But then she remembered again the anxiety of the moment. Her smile vanished, and she looked straight ahead.

The guerrillas were determined to keep their word. We heard them talking as they placed the dynamite around the passage. I was trying to think. I sat next to LaCrosse and said, shortly: "Look, we are all going up if we don't think of something. Is there a way to get to another wing of the castle?"

LaCrosse didn't have my scruples. He spoke loud and clear. "Perhaps there is. But I am not interested in escaping. Everything I ever dreamed of is in this castle. I will go to hell with all the objects of a lifetime's passions. There are other rooms in this castle...." His face took on a dreamy expression. "There are rooms here the combined authorities of church and state would give millions to recover...."

I was struck by his insane satisfactions. Then something occurred to me. "Is the Loire cup here?"

LaCrosse studied me with an amused smile. "Yes."

In spite of everything, I felt a certain awesome respect for the man. He seemed to be, in many ways, a mad poet who, like me once upon a time, had dreamed of imprisoning the world in his art. His art was this castle full of treasures.

"LaCrosse, I am not a moralist. I do not find you entirely despicable. I want to ask something of you. It is the last thing I will ask of anyone apparently.... Can we see it?"

LaCrosse looked at me intently. There was no sympathy in his gaze. He merely studied me like an insect.

"You want to see it.... You must know something: This wing of the castle was inhabited by Hunyadi, the Hungarian prince. He built this wing entirely for pleasure. There is no escape from here. If I show you the chalice, you will not be able to get away. If they use enough dynamite, the result will be the same.... Don't try anything stupid...."

I promised.

He motioned to his ropes. I untied his feet. I thought it safer to keep his hands tied behind his back. He rose majestically. With all due credit to the man, he had the bearing of a "cardinal." The robe he wore fit the severe symmetry of his bearing.

"LaCrosse leads the way," I said. "Lorraine, you walk behind him. Girls, you walk in a single line behind Lorraine. André and Derrain, walk behind the girls. I will be the last."

We untied André and Derrain's feet and, one by one, we filed through the girls' bedroom into a small antechamber. A small wooden door, bolted shut, stood to one side.

"The key is around my neck," said LaCrosse.

I took it and opened the lock. Lorraine drew the bolts.

"This is where I sleep," LaCrosse said simply. He could have said, "This is the king" with the same simplicity.

My eyes had a hard time adjusting to the extraordinary vision of this perfectly round room. Everyone else gasped. No one had, until this time, seen this room. It was dominated by an extraordinary statue of a crucifixion. Arranged in what seemed to be a curious pattern (I realized, much later, that the pattern was a pentagram, the kind used in witchcraft) were a number of religious objects. I did not know at the time that these were all objects that had played a central role in the major religious miracles of our century. But I sensed, even without knowing, that they were charged with an uncanny power. And finally, sitting on a simple red velvet pedestal, was the cup of Loire or the cup of Persephone, the extraordinary erotic object of antiquity.

I cannot describe this object without failing. I have tried a number of times. Every time I feel a curious emotion and I become speechless. Perhaps, one day, I will be able to. As it is, I must be content to say that, indeed, this chalice had been in the hand of an ancient goddess, it had dazzled the folks of Loire and it took away the breath of everyone in the room. Even André and Derrain, who, up to this point, had displayed a total lack of interest in the drama, looked moved. The girls fell absolutely silent.

It was Lorraine who spoke first. "We can't…. We must give ourselves up…."

Under the spell of the chalice I had formulated the same thought. We could not allow these treasures and especially the sacred cup of Persephone to go up in flames. Our lives weren't worth it.

But soon I began thinking again. "The guerrillas don't know about the existence of these objects.... They are worth millions; they cannot afford to lose them for their organization.... There is enough here to buy weapons for ten armies...."

Proceeding in the same order, we filed back. When we returned to the first room, I realized, to my horror, that we had no watch. I shouted to the door: "We must talk!"

But nothing moved on the other side. Our time of grace had, apparently, elapsed as we were gawking at the chalice, unaware. The guerrillas were gone. The only sound coming from the other side of the blocked passage door was the dreadful tick of a time device.

Back, we must get back to the room. We were not so vulnerable in there. Immediately, we proceeded the way we came and entered the round room once more. I shut the door.

Huddled like this around the sacred cup, we seemed like an ancient picture in an illuminated manuscript; some ancient drama seemed to be unfolding. Lorraine put her head on my shoulder.

LaCrosse had a triumphant and ironic expression on his face. In a strange way, he seemed to be at peace. His madness would be finally resolved in death.

The armored cars crawled grimly up the mountain. Myra had been feeling very tense for the past few minutes. She watched the snowy peaks with a concentration that was almost inhuman. Then the shots startled her. The column had stopped. Something was going on.

The waiting was unbearable. Finally, Colonel Lammai come running toward their car.

"We have the guerrillas," he said.

Myra and Giacomo jumped out of the car and ran up to the front of the column. Three men with their arms behind their heads, their palms crossed in the air, stood against the command car. A soldier had their weapons strung over his shoulder—three machine guns.

Giacomo walked toward them with Myra panting behind. A Rumanian officer stopped him.

"You cannot speak to them."

"We must know what they have done to their hostages! Two!" Giacomo held his fingers in the air. "Two! Two hostages!"

There was a brief consultation between the officer and Colonel Lammai. Giacomo was allowed to approach the prisoners.

"Where are Lorraine and Brandon?" Giacomo asked Silvio, grabbing him suddenly by the ears and bringing his head down with a sharp movement onto the hood of the car. "You must tell me now!"

Wincing, Silvio pointed up. Myra followed the direction of his chin and saw the castle. Extraordinary!

Giacomo let go of the guerrilla.

Suddenly, there were a number of explosions and giant stones came tumbling down. Everyone dived for cover under the cars. Giacomo grabbed Silvio again and, using him as a shield, began climbing the slope, dodging stones and debris.

"This is the best hotel in Bucharest," said Myra. "I called room service six times and no one came up!" She smiled. She was holding Lorraine very tightly and rocking her back and forth like a baby.

I surveyed the scene with satisfaction. How I

loved them! I would have loved to go up and join them, but the cast on my broken arm really hurt.

Giacomo walked into the room.

"Can't you ever knock?" said Myra.

"Well, have they found him?" I asked.

"Not a trace."

"It's really a pity you didn't see it, Myra!"

"I don't care, love. You're the real treasure. Seeing you is worth more than any piece of junk."

"She's right, though, Myra." I said dreamily, "You should have seen it!"

"I have a feeling," said Giacomo, "that we will never see it. Nor will we ever see LaCrosse again."

I still could not make sense of LaCrosse's disappearance. It had been as mysterious as the fact that we were still alive. In the confusion of the blast I had looked only at Lorraine. When the dust cleared and I saw that everyone was alive, I did not even think of LaCrosse. Only later, when Giacomo had arrived with Silvio, I looked around for LaCrosse. He was nowhere to be seen, and neither was the chalice. The chamber was as round as ever, and even though part of the wall had collapsed, it had held against the dynamite. There was no secret passage to be seen. But, of course, given the incredible craft of those ancient architects, nothing was impossible.

"What now?" I asked Giacomo.

"Now I will take a vacation. Flora and Carlo have been arrested in Rome; I will go to Istanbul."

We looked at each other. What were we going to do? We felt so happy we didn't really consider the question yet.

FOURTEEN

Through the multicolored haze in their champagne glasses, Maria, Paolo, Giovanni and Alonso listened to the remnants of our story with unadulterated pride.

"I can't believe it," said Paolo. "You are truly extraordinary, Lorraine. Our film will gross ten million dollars,"

"Money, money," said Maria. "Is that all you can think about?"

"I'm so happy, I *have* to think about money," said Paolo shrugging his shoulders in typical Italian.

Lorraine laughed. She was wearing a very décoleté girl-scout uniform in which she looked about ten; a yellow bandana was tied around her left ankle and her girlish knees thrust forward over the edge of the armchair in a classic Lorraine pose: her feet over the arms, her arms akimbo over the top of it.

"Yeah, I guess I'm a tough chick," she said.

"I still don't understand how Giacomo found out where they were holding you...." said Alonso.

"He was on the train to Rumania with Brandon. He also got off when the guerrillas stopped the train. He didn't follow them for fear they would notice. But next day he studied the area and realized the existence of the castle."

"How did he explore without a car?" asked Maria.

"A mule," Myra laughed.

Next day, we woke early. On the dresser was a little envelope. I picked it up and looked at it. It was another installment of fifty thousand dollars from Paolo. The message inside said simply: recasting.

We lulled in bed, eating breakfast. It was just like old times ... or was it? I knew certain things had changed. I looked at Lorraine. In spite of her same youthful appearance, I knew that she had matured enormously in the past few weeks. She appeared or tried to appear just as frivolous as she had always been, but there was something else there, a quiet seriousness of sorts.... I knew that, in her head, she was thinking about a lot of things.

Myra, too, confided this in her diary:

What a difference between our first time in Rome and this! When we first came here we were so childish. Lorraine's slave bracelets! I feel like crying. We were full of romantic illusions. I was looking for the chalice, Lorraine was looking for life. But now ... I know the chalice was only a pretext. How much we all have changed. Brandon will probably write his story, but it will be so different from what he imagined.

Later, we were still in bed when Giovanni Creghi called. He burst into the room, cursing: "The Communists don't want the story anymore, *per il sangre di Dio*.... I would have left out all the Rumanian parts, too.... I have no choice but to write a book and pretend it's fiction...."

"Brandon is writing that book," said Myra.

"Oh, no," I said, "I'm writing a totally different book. For an extra little sum we can agree on the rights to this *fiction*.... It's everybody's story...."

Myra laughed. "You're not a bad businessman, Brandon!"

Creghi began to complain ecstatically: "You're going to ruin me, *per la madonna!*"

But eventually he agreed.

Telephone calls and letters poured in. It was amazing that all these many people had been able to keep the whole affair secret. Rumors, of course, had been flying, but nothing had as yet surfaced in the press.

Holding the receiver in her hand, Myra looked about to have a fit. She kept making little circles with her fingers in my direction.

"What was that all about?" I asked when she finally put the phone back.

"Oh, Brandon, it's really incredible.... The Church wants to decorate us ... *discreetly*...."

I laughed. "The order of St. George?"

"It's so funny," said Myra. "I'm proud that they have recovered the six relics. The cup, of course ..."

Lorraine looked up. "You should have seen it, love...." She seemed depressed.

"Is it the letters from home?"

"Yup."

Pop wasn't writing to her anymore; it was Mom's turn. Two uncles wrote, too. Mom had this to say:

I saw a movie of a car accident at my Driver's Education class. A man was caught in the door of his car and dragged to death over twelve miles of asphalt with both his feet bleeding and his hand hanging from a single tendon through a hole in the door. I sure hope some of my kids will make something of themselves someday. Don't forget to write your Uncle Harry, he's dying of cancer of the leg—I sure hope you don't smoke—and he would appreciate a note before he goes. Also, a get-well card would be appreciated for poor Father Callaghan, who christened you and now is so swollen with hydrophobia he weighs four hundred pounds and they had to enlarge the confessional.

The news from Dubuque was a little wacky, to say the least. But it saddened Lorraine nevertheless.

"You should be glad they don't know what you were really up to!" I said.

I looked out the window. There were signs of autumn in the air. I couldn't exactly put my finger on it, but looking at the first drifting leaves, I had the distinct feeling that soon we would take separate paths and become, once more, three single individuals.

That Myra was feeling it too became evident a little later. We were sitting in a café, drinking wine after an incredibly great dinner, talking leisurely.

"I foresee a change with autumn...." I said. "Maybe it's just the usual melancholy.... But you have to return to Ann Arbor, Lorraine...." I looked at her. "What are you going to do, Lorraine?"

"I don't know," she said. "Maria wants me to be

an actress. She said she would pay for my studies....
She says I have star quality. But I don't know ... I
think I would like to go back to school...."

We fell silent. The wind rattled the windowpanes.

"Perhaps there was a plan to all this...." I began
again. "Perhaps my meeting with Dreyfus wasn't
accidental...."

"Perhaps," said Myra. "Did I ever tell you that
once I was part of another threesome?"

I was surprised. "No, tell us...."

"Well, I was rather new at this sort of thing back
then, and it took a lot of working out. I was sleeping
with Victor Torso and feeling very guilty about it. I
confessed everything to my husband and, you know
how he is, he decided that we might turn our situation to some scientific advantage. He suggested that I
pick myself a new lover to assist me on a trek of
detective pornography. At the time, the Psychology
Department was involved in a study of sexual attitudes and was chaired by a good friend of ours. The
deal was for me and my young man to go to France
and look up rare erotica as well as report on our sexual intimacy, the guilt, etcetera. It was a collaboration
between the Psychology and the History Departments...."

"You mean to tell me," I said, "that two presti-
gious departments of a reputed ..."

"Exactly, dear. Two respected departments got
together to finance the seven-year-itch of a frustrated
professor's wife! But that wasn't all.... There were
complications. The young man I picked happened to
be married, and I really liked his wife. I liked her, in
fact, better than I liked him at first. The three of us set
up a ménage à trois in Paris. We didn't last the three

months we had been given. Every shade of jealousy appeared.... We opted out. But that was only a little vacation.... It is all different now."

"How?" asked Lorraine.

"Well, for one thing, I love both of you deeply. We went through so much...."

"Look," said Lorraine, "maybe you guys are an older generation.... Guilt and all that.... If I want to fuck somebody, I fuck them ... even if there are three people...."

"You play tougher than you are, love." I smiled at her. "You're pretty attached to this band. You play pretty good flute, too...."

"Flute?! I play the piano!"

"Now, now, don't get into a fight!"

We didn't.

But I saw Lorraine's point. Maybe we were of a different generation. I blushed to think of my original intention to build a woman in *my* story. What amazing arrogance! Both Myra and I had had ulterior motives, subterfuges and pretexts! Myra had justified much of her adventure through her "research." I, through my Great Story. Only Lorraine needed no pretext for being around and enjoying herself. Myra and I had been perverted by our upbringings. We both wanted to believe that we were here to signify something, to stand for something. Lorraine, on the other hand, stood just as she was. For her we were time itself. To me....

Myra snapped the thread of my overrunning sensibility. "Do we have any more business in Italy?"

"No business, love, just pleasure."

And that was very much what—for the next two

weeks—we had. I could, of course, detail the hours we spent in a kind of sensual stupor in the lush opportunities of our remaining time. But I prefer to keep them secret, although I am sure that when Creghi's book comes out it will be filled with all kinds of revolting and delicious details.

It is in light of the generous wealth of pleasure we experienced that I would like to understand Lorraine's consequent repentance.

In some ways, I understood her decision to return to school in Ann Arbor and pursue a career in business. After all, she perhaps wasn't cut out for the emotional nonsense of acting.

What I don't understand and probably never will is the reason for her sexual repentance. The reason for her distance toward us, her coldness. After all, we had shared a lot.

Could the terrorists, in spite of themselves, have instilled a certain righteousness in Lorraine? After all, they had been dedicated young people. Several times I tried to approach Lorraine on the subject, but she refused to talk about it.

My argument, to which she did not reply, was simply that I could find it impossible to live in a world where I felt useful and used by society every minute. I have no doubt that, sooner or later, the world will be ruled by an iron hand (or lung) for its own good. But why hurry toward such drab days? I wanted to feel free to experience. It would be a sorry day indeed when I regarded my life from the point of view of factory management. I would be useless to myself then.

The only clue I have is the last night in Rome. We had been out dancing that night, and when we returned, both Myra and I felt very amorous. We were kissing and playfully clawing each other, trying to draw Lorraine into our circle, but she remained aloof. Myra and I went to bed and played, pretending to moan deeply and breathing heavily and carrying on with other such playful nonsense. But Lorraine still wouldn't go for it. So we made love, a little sadly, I thought, and waited for her. Lorraine was sitting in a chair reading a *History of Transylvania*. It was the first serious book I ever remember her holding.

"The Bermuda Triangle is opening franchises," I said, referring to Lorraine's disappearance from the common bed.

"Do you think she's repentant?" I whispered to Myra when Lorraine gave no sign of wanting to answer. It was the first time I mentioned the word which had begun to dominate my thoughts.

"Have you ever repented, Myra?" I asked.

"Of many things, but never of this...."

"Of stupid things, of course...."

"Do you feel any guilt, Brandon?"

I searched my soul. Truly I didn't. Love is what I felt. Nowhere in the vast flats of my psychological makeup did I feel any guilt.

"No."

"How can you write, then?" joked Myra. "Norman Mailer says you need guilt to write."

"That may be the problem. I haven't written a word since we met."

We sat for a few minutes in silence, drifting off to sleep.

"I miss my family," said Myra sleepily.

Under our windows, a drunk went by singing *La*

Bandiera Rossa, the Communist hymn. But Lorraine still didn't come to bed.

It was raining in Dubuque when we landed. Before entrusting Lorraine to the safekeeping of her family, the three of us shared coffee at a roadside diner. It was a sweet farewell. Autumn was already in full swing, putting a deep touch of melancholy on us. Leaves were falling outside, floating slowly amid the traffic.

"WHY DON'T GOD ORDAIN THINGS DIFFER-ENTLY?" the old woman screamed, and, at that moment, I felt that a veil fell from Lorraine's face. I could almost see two lines beginning to form at the corners of her mouth. She was growing older on the spot.

The waitress gave the old woman at the counter a sour look, and I felt a great weight in my heart.

"I'm sorry," Lorraine said, addressing herself half to the old woman's mysterious plight and half to us.

We finished the coffee. There was nothing left to do except put Lorraine on the blue city bus and kiss her. Unquestionably, we still desired each other. It couldn't end; how could it? Only boredom ends love, and this wasn't, certainly, our problem.

Before the doors on the bus closed, Lorraine hand-ed me a thick white envelope.

"I don't want the money!" she said.

"Lorraine!" But the bus was gone.

Even if I weren't a writer, I would give all the cash in that envelope (a sizable amount) to anyone who could accurately supply what went on in Lorraine's head during that bus ride.

In Ann Arbor, every light was blazing in the Kaminski household. The taxi deposited us there, and we climbed the stairs.

During the flood of affectionate kisses that broke in a mini-storm around Myra, I studied her two daughters. I had never seen them before. They clustered around their travel-weary mother like two young furies. They were as pretty as you please, two blossoms not much younger than Lorraine.

"Instructive?" asked V. Torso, lighting his pipe.

"Confusing," I said.

"Life, friend, is confusing. Did you write your story?"

At this point, Dr. Kaminski and Dr. Collins broke away from Myra to shake my hand. The good doctor seemed pleased to see me.

"You have taken good care of my wife," he said, stroking his ambiguous Vandyke. "She doesn't look a day older; she looks a summer younger."

I looked at Myra being adored on the couch. It wasn't true; she looked very tired indeed. Who were all these people? I bid my good-byes and left. I was going to stay in a motel.

Outside, the autumn had gathered its big chilly stars in a tight rostrum over my head. A tiny shadow was trying to catch up with me. My heart quickened. I felt very weary of shadows.

It was Lolita.

"I expected you to be through with the important people by now...." She walked alongside me, her girlish body swinging in rhythm with mine.

"How is school?" I said.

"Aw, jinx!"

"How is you job?"

"Oh, did you know that old Doc Kaminski is a sex weirdo?"

"How so?"

"He collects all the stuff...."

"And?"

"When he makes love, he'll like spread my legs and say weird things like 'No trace remains of Stevenson's honeymoon hovel,' or he'll be talking to his cock and saying 'Memo to the merry Mormon.'"

"No kidding!"

"You know what?"

"What?"

"Remember the pimply kid?"

"Yeah."

"He's gone bananas. He's become an artist. He dropped out of school and lives now in a studio that's covered with these paintings and drawings of Lorraine ... from memory."

"Wow! That bad?"

"Don't laugh at me," Lolita said, taking my arm. "I have a little apartment. You'll like it."

People are talking about:

The Masquerade Erotic Newsletter

◆ ◆ ◆ ◆ ◆ ◆ ◆ ◆ ◆ ◆ ◆ ◆ ◆ ◆ ◆ ◆ ◆ ◆

FICTION, ESSAYS, REVIEWS, PHOTOGRAPHY, INTERVIEWS, EXPOSÉS, AND MUCH MORE!

◆ ◆ ◆ ◆ ◆ ◆ ◆ ◆ ◆ ◆ ◆ ◆ ◆ ◆ ◆ ◆ ◆ ◆

"I received the new issue of the newsletter; it looks better and better."
—*Michael Perkins*

"I must say that yours is a nice little magazine, literate and intelligent."
—*HH, Great Britain*

"Fun articles on writing porn and about the peep shows, great for those of us who will probably never step onto a strip stage or behind the glass of a booth, but love to hear about it, wicked little voyeurs that we all are, hm? Yes indeed...."
—*MT, California*

"Many thanks for your newsletter with essays on various forms of eroticism. Especially enjoyed your new Masquerade collections of books dealing with gay sex."
—*GF, Maine*

"... a professional, insider's look at the world of erotica ..."
—*SCREW*

"I recently received a copy of **The Masquerade Erotic Newsletter**. I found it to be quite informative and interesting. The intelligent writing and choice of subject matter are refreshing and stimulating. You are to be congratulated for a publication that looks at different forms of eroticism without leering or smirking."
—*DP, Connecticut*

"Thanks for sending the books and the two latest issues of **The Masquerade Erotic Newsletter**. Provocative reading, I must say."
—*RH, Washington*

"Thanks for the latest copy of **The Masquerade Erotic Newsletter**. It is a real stunner."
—*CJS, New York*

Free
GIFT

PRIVATE LESSONS   *Lindsay Welsh*

A high voltage tale of life at The Whitfield Academy for Young Women—where cruel headmistress Devon Whitfield presides over the in-depth education of only the most talented and delicious of maidens. Elizabeth Dunn arrives at the Academy, where it becomes clear that she has much to learn—to the delight of Devon Whitfield and her randy staff of Mistresses in Residence!   **3116-0**

BAD HABITS   *Lindsay Welsh*

What does one do with a poorly trained slave? Break her of her bad habits, of course! When a respected dominatrix notices the poor behavior displayed by her slave, she decides to open a school: one where submissives will learn the finer points of servitude—and learn them properly. "If you like hot, lesbian erotica, run—don't walk ... and pick up a copy of *Bad Habits* ..."   —Karen Bullock-Jordan, *Lambda Book Report*. **3068-7**

PROVINCETOWN SUMMER   *Lindsay Welsh*

This completely original collection is devoted exclusively to white-hot desire between women.From the casual encounters of women on the prowl to the enduring erotic bond between old lovers, the women of *Provincetown Summer* will set your senses on fire! A nationally bestselling title.   **3040-7**

MISTRESS MINE   *Valentina Cilescu*

Sophia Cranleigh sits in prison, accused of authoring the "obscene" *Mistress Mine*. She is offered salvation—with the condition that she first relate her lurid life story. For Sophia has led no ordinary life, but has slaved and suffered—deliciously—under the hand of the notorious Mistress Malin. Sophia tells her story, never imagining the way in which she'd be repaid for her honesty....   **109-8**

LEATHERWOMEN   *edited by Laura Antoniou*

A groundbreaking anthology. These fantasies, from the pens of new or emerging authors, break every rule imposed on women's fantasies, telling stories of the secret extremes so many dream of. The hottest stories from some of today's newest and most outrageous writers make this an unforgettable exploration of the female libido.   **3095-4**

PASSAGE AND OTHER STORIES   *Aarona Griffin*

An S/M romance. Lovely Nina is frightened by her lesbian passions until she finds herself infatuated with a woman she spots at a local café. One night Nina follows her and finds herself enmeshed in an endless maze leading to a mysterious world where women test the edges of sexuality and power.   **3057-1**

DISTANT LOVE & OTHER STORIES   *A.L. Reine*

In the title story, Leah Michaels and her lover Ranelle have had four years of blissful, smoldering passion together. One night, when Ranelle is out of town, Leah records an audio "Valentine," a cassette filled with erotic reminiscences of their life together in vivid, pulsating detail.   **3056-3**

EROTIC *PLAYGIRL* ROMANCES
$4.95 each

WOMEN AT WORK *Charlotte Rose*

Hot, uninhibited stories devoted to the working woman! From a lonesome cowgirl to a supercharged public relations exec, these uncontrollable women know how to let off steam after a tough day on the job. Career pursuits pale beside their devotion to less professional pleasures, as each proves that "moonlighting" is often the best job of all! **3088-1**

LOVE & SURRENDER *Marlene Darcy*

"Madeline saw Harry looking at her legs and she blushed as she remembered what he wanted to do.... She casually pulled the skirt of her dress back to uncover her knees and the lower part of her thighs. What did he want now? Did he want more? She tugged at her skirt again, pulled it back far enough so almost all of her thighs were exposed...." **3082-2**

THE COMPLETE *PLAYGIRL* FANTASIES

The very best—and very hottest—women's fantasies are collected here, fresh from the pages of *Playgirl*. These knockouts from the infamous "Reader's Fantasy Forum" prove, once again, that truth can indeed be hotter, wilder, and *better* than fiction. **3075-X**

DREAM CRUISE *Gwenyth James*

Angelia has it all—a brilliant career and a beautiful face to match. But she longs to kick up her high heels and have some fun, so she takes an island vacation and vows to leave her sexual inhibitions behind. From the moment her plane takes off, she finds herself in one hot and steamy encounter after another, and her horny holiday doesn't end on Monday morning! Rest and relaxation were never so rewarding. **3045-0**

RHINO*CEROS* BOOKS
$6.95 each

RHINO*CEROS* ANTHOLOGY OF CLASSIC ANONYMOUS EROTIC WRITING *Edited by Michael Perkins*

Michael Perkins, acclaimed authority on erotic literature, has collected the very best passages from the world's erotic writing—especially for Rhino*ceros* readers. "Anonymous" is one of the most infamous bylines in publishing history—and these steamy excerpts show why! Well-crafted and arousing reading for porn connoisseurs. Available only from Rhino*ceros* Books. **140-3**

THE REPENTENCE OF LORRAINE *Andrei Codrescu*

An aspiring writer, a professor's wife, a secretary, gold anklets, Maoists, Roman harlots—and more—swirl through this spicy tale of a harried quest for a mythic artifact. Written when the author was a young man, this lusty yarn was inspired by the heady—and hot—days and nights of the Sixties. A rare title from this perenially popular and acclaimed author, finally back in print. **124-1**

THE WET FOREVER *David Aaron Clark*

The story of Janus and Madchen—a small-time hood and a beautiful sex worker—*The Wet Forever* examines themes of loyalty, sacrifice, redemption and obsession amidst Manhattan's sex parlors and underground S/M clubs.. Its combination of sex and suspense makes *The Wet Forever* singular, uncompromising, and strangely arousing. **117-9**

ORF *David Meltzer*

He is the ultimate musician-hero—the idol of thousands, the fevered dream of many more. And like many musicians before him, he is misunderstood, misused—and totally out of control. From agony to lust, every last drop of feeling is squeezed from a modern-day troubadour and his lady love on their relentless descent into hell. Long out of print, Meltzer's frank, poetic look at the dark side of the Sixties returns. A masterpiece—and a must for every serious erotic library. **110-1**

MANEATER *Sophie Galleymore Bird*

Through a bizarre act of creation, a man attains the "perfect" lover—by all appearances a beautiful, sensuous woman but in reality something far darker. Once brought to life she will accept no mate, seeking instead the prey that will sate her supernatural hunger for vengeance. A biting take on the war of the sexes, this stunning debut novel goes for the jugular of the "perfect woman" myth. **103-9**

VENUS IN FURS *Leopold von Sacher-Masoch*

This classic 19th century novel is the first uncompromising exploration of the dominant/submissive relationship in literature. The alliance of Severin and Wanda epitomizes Sacher-Masoch's dark obsession with a cruel, controlling goddess and the urges that drive the man held in her thrall. Also included in this volume are the letters exchanged between Sacher-Masoch and Emilie Mataja—an aspiring writer he sought as the avatar of his forbidden desires. **3089-X**

ALICE JOANOU

TOURNIQUET **3067-9**

A brand new collection of stories and effusions from the pen of one our most dazzling young writers. By turns lush and austere, Joanou's intoxicating command of language and image make *Tourniquet* a sumptuous feast for all the senses. From the writer *Screw* credited with making "the most impressive erotic debut in many a moon."

CANNIBAL FLOWER **72-6**

"She is waiting in her darkened bedroom, as she has waited throughout history, to seduce and ultimately destroy the men who are foolish enough to be blinded by her irresistible charms. She is Salome, Lucrezia Borgia, Delilah—endlessly alluring, the fulfillment of your every desire.... She is the goddess of sexuality, and *Cannibal Flower* is her haunting siren song." —Michael Perkins

MICHAEL PERKINS

EVIL COMPANIONS **3067-9**

A handsome edition of this cult classic that includes a new preface by Samuel R. Delany. Set in New York City during the tumultuous waning years of the 60s, *Evil Companions* has been hailed as "a frightening classic." A young couple explore the nether reaches of the erotic unconscious in a shocking confrontation with the extremes of passion. About *Evil Companions*, Thomas M. Disch said "Michael Perkins is America's answer to de Sade ... by comparison to this book, Bret Easton Ellis' *American Psycho* is only a lesson in good grooming...."

THE SECRET RECORD: Modern Erotic Literature **3039-3**

Michael Perkins, a renowned author and critic of sexually explicit fiction, surveys the field with authority and unique insight. Updated and revised to include the latest trends, tastes, and developments in this much-misunderstood and maligned genre. An important nonfiction volume for every erotic reader aand fan of high quality adult fiction, *The Secret Record* is finally back in print.

SENSATIONS *Tuppy Owens*

A piece of porn history. Tuppy Owens tells the unexpurgated story of the making of *Sensations*—the first big-budget sex flick. Originally commissioned to appear in book form after the release of the film in 1975, *Sensations* is finally released under Masquerade's stylish Rhino*ceros* imprint. A document from a more reckless, bygone time! **3081-4**

THE MARKETPLACE *Sara Adamson*

"Merchandise does not come easily to the Marketplace.... They haunt the clubs and the organizations, their need so real and desperate that they exude sensual tension when they glide through the crowds. Some of them are so ripe that they intimidate the poseurs, the weekend sadists and the furtive dilettantes who are so endemic to that world. And they never stop asking where we may be found...." A compelling tale of the ultimate training academy, where only the finest are accepted—and trained for service beyond their wildest dreams. **3096-2**

MY DARLING DOMINATRIX *Grant Antrews*

When a man and a woman fall in love it's supposed to be simple, uncomplicated, easy—unless that woman happens to be a dominatrix. Devoid of sleaze and shame, this honest and unpretentious love story captures the richness and depth of this very special kind of love. Rare and undeniably unique. **3055-5**

ILLUSIONS *Daniel Vian*

Two disturbing tales of danger and desire on the eve of WWII. From private homes to lurid cafés to decaying streets, passion is explored, exposed, and placed in stark contrast to the brutal violence of the time. *Illusions* peels the frightened mask from the face of desire, and studies its changing features under the dim lights of a lonely Berlin evening. Two unforgettable and evocative stories. **3074-1**

LOVE IN WARTIME *Liesel Kulig*

Madeleine knew that the handsome SS officer was a dangerous man. But she was just a cabaret singer in Nazi-occupied Paris, trying to survive in a perilous time. When Josef fell in love with her, he discovered that a beautiful and amoral woman can sometimes be wildly dangerous. **3044-X**

MASQUERADE BOOKS
$4.95 each

THE EROTIC ADVENTURES OF HARRY TEMPLE *Anonymous*

The first book of libertine Harry Temple's memoirs chronicles his amorous adventures from his initiation at the hands of two insatiable sirens, through his apprenticeship at a house of hot repute, to his encounters with a nymphomaniac in a chastity belt and other twisted partners. **127-6**

PAULINE *Anonymous*

From rural America to the Franfurt Opera House to the royal court of Austria, Pauline follows her ever growing sexual desires. "They knew not that I was a prima donna, sought after by royalty, indulged and petted by the elite of all Europe. I would never see them again. Why shouldn't I give myself to them that they might become more and more inspired to deeds of greater lust!" A sexy diva takes on all comers. **129-2**

ODD WOMEN *Rachel Perez*

These women are lots of things: sexy, smart, innocent, tough—some even say odd. But who cares, when their combined ass-ettes are so sweet! There's not a moral in sight as an assortment of Sapphic sirens proves once and for all that comely ladies come best in pairs. **123-3**

AFFINITIES *Rachel Perez*

"Kelsy had a liking for cool upper-class blondes, the long-legged girls from Lake Forest and Winnetka who came into the city to cruise the lesbian bars on Halsted, looking for breathless ecstasies. Kelsy thought of them as icebergs that needed melting, these girls with a quiet demeanor and so much under the surface...." **3113-6**

JENNIFER *Anonymous*

From the bedroom of an internationally famous—and notoriously insatiable—dancer to an uninhibited ashram, *Jennifer* traces the exploits of one thoroughly modern woman. Moving beyond mere sexual experimentation, Jennifer slowly comes to a new realization of herself—as a passionate woman whose hungers are as boundless as they are diverse. Nothing stops the insatiable Jennifer! **107-1**

HELLFIRE *Charles G. Wood*

A vicious murderer is running amok in New York's sexual underground—and Nick O'Shay, a virile detective with the NYPD, plunges deep into the case. He soon becomes embroiled in an elusive world of fleshly extremes, hunting a madman seeking to purge America with fire and blood sacrifices. But the rules are different here, as O'Shay soon discovers on his journey through every sexual extreme—and his ultimate encounter with the ugly face of repression. **3085-7**

ROSEMARY LANE *J.D. Hall*

The ups, downs, ins and outs of Rosemary Lane, an 18th century maiden named after the street in which she was abandoned as a child. Raised as the ward of Lord and Lady D'Arcy, after coming of age she discovers that her guardians' generosity is truly boundless—as they contribute heartily to her carnal education. **3078-4**

HELOISE *Sarah Jackson*

A panoply of sensual tales harkening back to the golden age of Victorian erotica. Desire is examined in all its intricacy, as fantasies are explored and urges explode. Innocence meets experience time and again in these passionate stories dedicated to the pleasures of the body. Sweetly torrid tales of erotic awakening abound in this volume devoted to the deepest sexual explorations. **3073-3**

MASTER OF TIMBERLAND *Sara H. French*

"Welcome to Timberland Resort," he began. "We are delighted that you have come to serve us. And you may all be assured that we will require service of you in the strictest sense. Our discipline is the most demanding in the world. You will be trained here by the best. And now your new Masters will make their choices." Luscious slaves serve in the ultimate vacation paradise. **3059-8**

GARDEN OF DELIGHT *Sydney St. James*

A vivid account of sexual awakening that follows an innocent but insatiably curious young woman's journey from the furtive, forbidden joys of dormitory life to the unabashed carnality of the wild world. Pretty Pauline blossoms with each new experiment in the sensual arts—until finally nothing can contain her extravagant desires. **3058-X**

STASI SLUT *Anthony Bobarzynski*

Adina lives in East Germany, far from the sexually liberated, uninhibited debauchery of the West. She meets a group of ruthless and corrupt STASI agents who use her as a pawn in their political chess game as well as for their own gratification—until she uses her undeniable talents and attractions in a final bid for total freedom in the revolutionary climax of this *Red*-hot thriller! **3052-0**

BLUE TANGO *Hilary Manning*

Ripe and tempting Julie is haunted by the sounds of extraordinary passion beyond her bedroom wall. Alone, she fantasizes about taking part in the amorous dramas of her hosts, Claire and Edward. When she finds a way to watch the nightly debauch, her curiosity turns to full-blown lust and the uncontrollable Julie goes wild with desire! **3037-7**

THE CATALYST *Sara Adamson*

After viewing a controversial, explicitly kinky film full of images of bondage and submission, several audience members find themselves deeply moved by the erotic suggestions they've seen on the screen. Each inspired coupling explores their every imagined extreme, as long-denied urges explode with new intensity. **3015-6**

LUST *Palmiro Vicarion*

A wealthy and powerful man of leisure recounts his rise up the corporate ladder and his corresponding descent into debauchery. Adventure and political intrigue provide a stimulating backdrop for this tale of a classic scoundrel with an uncurbed appetite for sexual power! **82-3**

WAYWARD *Peter Jason*

A mysterious countess hires a tour bus for an unusual vacation. Traveling through Europe's most notorious cities, she picks up friends, lovers, and acquaintances from every walk of life in pursuit of unbridled sensual pleasure. Each guest brings unique sexual tastes and talents to the group, climaxing in countless orgies, outrageous acts, endless deviation—and a trip none would forget! **3004-0**

ASK ISADORA *Isadora Alman*

Six years of collected columns on sex and relationships. Syndicated columnist Alman has been called a hip Dr. Ruth and a sexy Dear Abby. Her advice is sharp, funny, and pertinent to anyone experiencing the delights and dilemmas of being a sexual creature in today's perplexing world. **61-0**

LOUISE BELHAVEL

FORBIDDEN DELIGHTS

Clara and Iris make their sexual debut in this chronicle of the forbidden. Sexual taboos are what turn this pair on, as they travel the globe in search of the next erotic threshold. The effect they have on their fellow world travelers is definitely contagious! **81-5**

FRAGRANT ABUSES

The saga of Clara and Iris continues as the now-experienced girls enjoy themselves with a new circle of worldy friends whose imaginations definitely match their own. Polymorphous perversity follows the lusty ladies around the globe! **88-2**

DEPRAVED ANGELS

The final installment in the incredible adventures of Clara and Iris. Together with their friends, lovers, and worldly acquaintances, Clara and Iris explore the frontiers of depravity at home and abroad. **92-0**

TITIAN BERESFORD

A TITIAN BERESFORD READER

A captivating collection! Beresford's fanciful settings and outrageous fetishism have established his reputation as one of modern erotica's most imaginative and spirited writers. Wildly cruel dominatrixes, deliciously perverse masochists, and mesmerizing detail are the hallmarks of the Beresford tale—the best of which are collected here for the first time. **3114-4**

CINDERELLA

Titian Beresford triumphs again with castle dungeons and tightly corseted ladies-in-waiting, naughty viscounts and impossibly cruel masturbatrixes—nearly every conceivable method of erotic torture is explored and described in lush, vivid detail. **3024-5**

JUDITH BOSTON

Young Edward would have been lucky to get the stodgy old companion he thought his parents had hired for him. Instead, an exqusite woman arrives at his door, and Edward finds his compulsively lewd behavior never goes unpunished by the unflinchingly severe Judith Boston! **87-4**

CHINA BLUE

KUNG FU NUNS

"When I could stand the pleasure no longer, she lifted me out of the chair and sat me down on top of the table. She then lifted her skirt. The sight of her perfect legs clad in white stockings and a petite garter belt further mesmerized me. I lean particularly towards white garter belts." **3031-8**

SECRETS OF THE CITY

China Blue, the infamous Madame of Saigon, a black belt enchantress in the martial arts of love, is out for revenge. Her search brings her to Manhattan, where she intends to call upon her secret sexual arts to kill her enemies at the height of ecstasy. **03-3**

HARRIET DAIMLER

DARLING • INNOCENCE

In *Darling,* a virgin is raped by a mugger. Driven by her urge for revenge, she searches New York for him in a furious sexual hunt that leads to rape and murder. In *Innocence,* a young invalid determines to experience sex through her voluptuous nurse. Two critically acclaimed novels in one extraordinary volume. **3047-4**

THE PLEASURE THIEVES

They are the Pleasure Thieves, whose sexually preoccupied targets are set up by luscious Carol Stoddard. She forms an ultra-hot sexual threesome with them, trying every combination from two-on-ones to daisy chains—but always on the sly, because pleasures are even sweeter when they're stolen! **036-X**

AKBAR DEL PIOMBO

SKIRTS

Randy Mr. Edward Champdick enters high society—and a whole lot more—in his quest for ultimate satisfaction. For it seems that once Mr. Champdick rises to the occasion, almost nothing can bring him down. Nothing, that is, except continual, indiscriminate sexual gratification under the nearest skirt. **3115-2**

DUKE COSIMO

A kinky, lighthearted romp of non-stop action is played out against the boudoirs, bathrooms and ballrooms of the European nobility, who seem to do nothing all day except each other. **3052-0**

A CRUMBLING FAÇADE

The return of that incorrigible rogue, Henry Pike,who continues his pursuit of sex, fair or otherwise, in the most elegant homes of the most irreproachable and debauched aristocrats. No one can resist the irrespressible Pike—especially when he's on the prowl. **3043-1**

PAULA

"How bad do you want me?" she asked, her voice husky, breathy. I shrank back, for my desire for her was swelling to unspeakable proportions . "Turn around," she said, and I obeyed, willing to do as she asked.   **3036-9**

ROBERT DESMOND

PROFESSIONAL CHARMER

A gigolo lives a parasitical life of luxury by providing his sexual services to the rich and bored. Traveling in the most exclusive circles, this gun-for-hire will gratify the lewdest and most vulgar sexual cravings. Every exploit he performs is described in lurid, throbbing detail in this story of a prostitute's progress!   **3003-2**

THE SWEETEST FRUIT

Connie is determined to seduce and destroy Father Chadcrof. She corrupts the priest into forsaking all that he holds sacred, destroys his peaceful parish, and slyly manipulates him with her smoldering looks and hypnotic sexual aura.   **95-5**

MICHAEL DRAX

SILK AND STEEL

"He stood tall and strong in the shadows of her room … Akemi knew what he was there for. He let his robe fall to the floor. She could offer no resistance as the shadowy figure knelt before her, gazing down upon her. Why would she resist? This was what she wanted all along.…"   **3032-6**

OBSESSIONS

Victoria is determined to become a model by sexually ensnaring the powerful people who control the fashion industry: a voyeur who enjoys photographing Victoria as much as she enjoys teasing him; Paige, who finds herself compelled to watch Victoria's conquests; Pietro and Alex, who take turns and then join in for a sizzling threesome. Anything—and everything—goes!   **3012-1**

LIZBETH DUSSEAU

CAROLINE'S CONTRACT

After a long life of repression, Caroline goes out on a limb. On the advice of a friend, she meets with the dark and alluring Max Burton—a man more than willing to indulge her deepest fantasies of domination and discipline. Caroline soon learns to love the ministrations of Max—and agrees to a very *special* arrangement.…   **122-5**

MEMBER OF THE CLUB

"I wondered what would excite me … And deep down inside, I had the most submissive thoughts: I imagined myself … under the grip of men I hardly knew. If there were a club to join, it could take my deepest dreams and make them real. My only question was how far I'd really go?" A young woman faces the ultimate temptation—and finally goes all the way in a quest to satisfy her hungers.   **3079-2**

THE APPLICANT

"Adventuresome young woman who enjoys being submissive sought by married couple in early forties. Expect no limits." Hilary answers an ad, hoping to find someone who can meet her special needs. The beautiful Liza turns out to be a flawless mistress, and together with her husband Oliver, she trains Hilary to be the perfect servant. Unforgivably delicious sadism abounds.   **3038-5**

CAROUSEL

A young American woman leaves her husband when she discovers he is having an affair with their maid. She then becomes the sexual plaything of various Parisian voluptuaries. Wild sex, low morals, and ultimate decadence in the flamboyant years before the European collapse. **3051-2**

SABINE

One of the most unforgettable seductresses ever. There is no one who can refuse her once she casts her spell; no lover can do anything less than give up his whole life for her. Great men and empires fall at her feet; but she is haughty, distracted, impervious. It is the eve of WW II, and Sabine must find a new lover equal to her talents and her tastes. **3046-6**

THREE WOMEN

A knot of sexual dependence ties three women to each other and the men who love them. Dr. Helen Webber finds that her natural authority thrills and excites her lover Aaron. Jan, is involved in an affair with a married man whose wife eases her loneliness by slumming—and much more—at the local bar with the working guys. A torrid, tempestuous triangle reaches the boiling point! **3025-3**

THE WILD HEART

A luxury hotel is the setting for this artful web of sex, desire, and love. A newlywed sees sex as a duty, while her hungry husband tries to awaken her to its tender joys. A Parisian entertains the wealthy guests for the love of money. Each episode provides a delicious variation in this libidinal Grand Hotel! **3007-5**

DEMON HEAT

An ancient vampire stalks the unsuspecting in the form of a beautiful and utterly irresistable woman. Unlike the legendary Dracula, this fiend doesn't drink blood; she craves a different kind of potion. When her insatiable appetite has drained every last drop of juice from her victims, they hunger for more! **79-3**

HAREM SONG

Young, sensuous Amber flees her cruel uncle and provincial village in search of a better life, but finds she is no match for the glittering light of London. Soon Amber becomes a call girl and is sold into a lusty Sultan's harem—a vocation for which she possesses more than average talent, to her own surprise—and delight! **73-4**

JADE EAST

Laura, passive and passionate, follows her domineering husband Emilio to Hong Kong. He gives her to Wu Li, a Chinese connoisseur of sexual perversions, who passes her on to Madeleine, a flamboyant lesbian. Madeleine's friends make Laura the centerpiece in Hong Kong's underground orgies—where she watches Emilio recruit another lovely young woman. A journey into sexual slavery! **60-2**

RAWHIDE LUST

Diana Beaumont, the young wife of a U.S. Marshal, is kidnapped as an act of vengeance against her husband. Jack Beaumont sets out on a long journey to get his wife back, but finally catches up with her trail only to learn that she's been sold into white slavery in Mexico. **55-6**

THE JAZZ AGE

The time is the Roaring Twenties; A young attorney becomes suspicious of his mistress while his wife has an interlude with a lesbian lover. *The Jazz Age* is a romp of erotic realism from the heyday of the flapper and the speakeasy. **48-3**

EROTOMANIA

The bible of female sexual perversion! It's all here, everything you ever wanted to know about kinky women past and present. From simple nymphomania to the most outrageous fetishism, all secrets are revealed in this look into the forbidden rooms of feminine desire. Thoroughly sensational!   **128-4**

AN ALIZARIN LAKE READER

A selection of wicked musings from the pen of Masquerade's perennially popular author. It's all here: *Business as Usual, The Erotic Adventures of Harry Temple, Festival of Venus,* the mysterious *Instruments of the Passion,* the devilish *Miss High Heels*—and more. Each unforgettable moment of lust makes this a deliciously prurient page-turner!   **106-3**

SEX ON DOCTOR'S ORDERS

A chronicle of selfless devotion to mankind! Beth, a nubile young nurse, uses her considerable skills to further medical science by offering incomparable and insatiable assistance in the gathering of important specimens. No man leaves Nurse Beth's station without surrendering exactly what she needs! A guaranteed cure for all types of fever.   **3092-X**

MISS HIGH HEELS

It was a delightful punishment few men dared to dream of. Who could have predicted how far it would go? Forced by his wicked sisters to dress and behave like a proper lady, Dennis Beryl finds he enjoys life as Denise much more!   **3066-0**

THE INSTRUMENTS OF THE PASSION

All that remains is the diary of a young initiate, detailing the twisted rituals of a mysterious cult institution known only as "Rossiter." Behind sinister walls, a beautiful young woman performs an unending drama of pain and humiliation. What is the impulse that justifies her, night after night, in consenting to this strange ceremony? And to what lengths will her aberrant passion drive her?   **3010-5**

CLARA

The mysterious death of a beautiful, aristocratic woman leads her old boyfriend on an harrowing journey of discovery. His search uncovers a woman on a quest for deeper and more unusual sensations, each more shocking then the one before.   **80-7**

FESTIVAL OF VENUS

Brigeen Mooney fled her home in the west of Ireland to avoid being forced into a nunnery. But her refuge in Dublin turned out to be dedicated to a different religion. The women she met there belonged to the Old Religion, devoted to sex and sacrifices. Sex ceremonies of pagan gods!   **37-8**

PAUL LITTLE

THE DISCIPLINE OF ODETTE

Odette's family was harsh, but not even public humiliation could keep her from Jacques. She was sure marriage to him would rescue her from her family's "corrections." To her horror, she discovers that Jacques, too, has been raised on discipline. An explosive and shocking erotic coupling.   **3033-4**

ALL THE WAY

Two excruciating novels from Paul Little in one hot volume! *Going All the Way* features an unhappy man who tries to purge himself of the memory of his lover with a series of quirky and uninhibited women. *Pushover* tells the story of a serial spanker and his celebrated exploits in California.   **3023-7**

RICHARD KASAK BOOKS

LARRY TOWNSEND
ASK LARRY

Twelve years of Masterful advice (and the occasional command) from Larry Townsend (*Run, Little Leatherboy, Chains*), the leatherman's long-time confidant and adviser. Starting just before the onslaught of AIDS, Townsend wrote the "Leather Notebook" column for *Drummer* magazine, tackling subjects from sexual technique to safer sex, whips to welts, Daddies to dog collars. Now, with *Ask Larry*, readers can avail themselves of Townsend's collected wisdom as well as the author's contemporary commentary—a careful consideration of the way life has changed in the AIDS era, and the specific ways in which the disease has altered perceptions of once-simple problems. Any man worth his leathers can't afford to miss this volume from one of the tribe's most celebrated and trusted scribes. $12.95/289-2

RUSS KICK
OUTPOSTS:
A Catalog of Rare and Disturbing Alternative Information

A huge, authoritative guide to some of the most offbeat and bizarre publications available today! Dedicated to the notion of a society based on true freedom of expression, *Outposts* shines light into the darkest nooks and most overlooked crannies of American thought. Rather than simply summarize the plethora of controversial opinions crowding the American scene, Kick has tracked down the real McCoy and compiled over five hundred reviews of work penned by political extremists, conspiracy theorists, hallucinogenic pathfinders, sexual explorers, religious iconoclasts and social malcontents. Better yet, each review is followed by ordering information for the many readers sure to want these remarkable publications for themselves. $19.95/0202-8

WILLIAM CARNEY
THE REAL THING

Carney gives us a good look at the mores and lifestyle of the first generation of gay leathermen. A chilling mystery/romance novel as well.   —Pat Califia

Out of print for years, *The Real Thing* has long served as a touchstone in any consideration of gay "edge fiction." First published in 1968, this uncompromising story of New York leathermen received instant acclaim —and in the years since, has become a highly-prized volume to those lucky enough to acquire a copy. Now, *The Real Thing* returns from exile, ready to thrill a new generation—and reacquaint itself with its original audience. $10.95/280-9

LOOKING FOR MR. PRESTON

Edited by Laura Antoniou, *Looking for Mr. Preston* includes work by Lars Eighner, Pat Califia, Michael Bronski, Felice Picano, Joan Nestle, Larry Townsend, Sasha Alyson, Andrew Holleran, Michael Lowenthal, and others who contributed interviews, essays and personal reminiscences of John Preston—a man whose career spanned the industry from the early pages of the *Advocate* to various national bestseller lists. Preston was the author of over twenty books, including *Franny, the Queen of Provincetown*, and *Mr. Benson*. He also edited the noted *Flesh and the Word* erotic anthologies, *Personal Dispatches: Writers Confront AIDS*, and *Hometowns*,. More importantly, Preston became a personal inspiration, friend and mentor to many of today's gay and lesbian authors and editors. Ten percent of the proceeds from sale of the book will go to the AIDS Project of Southern Maine, for which Preston had served as President of the Board. $23.95/288-4

RICHARD KASAK BOOKS

AMARANTHA KNIGHT, EDITOR

LOVE BITES

A volume of tales dedicated to legend's sexiest demon—the Vampire. Amarantha Knight, herself an author who has delved into vampire lore, has gathered the very best writers in the field to produce a collection of uncommon, and chilling, allure. Including such names as Ron Dee, Nancy A. Collins, Nancy Kilpatrick, Lois Tilton and David Aaron Clark, *Love Bites* is not only the finest collection of erotic horror available—but a virtual who's who of promising new talent. $12.95/234-5

MICHAEL LOWENTHAL, EDITOR

THE BEST OF THE BADBOYS

A collection of the best of Masquerade Books' phenomenally popular Badboy line of gay erotic writing. Badboy's sizable roster includes many names that are legendary in gay circles. The very best of the leading Badboys is collected here, in this testament to the artistry that has catapulted these "outlaw" authors to bestselling status. John Preston, Aaron Travis, Larry Townsend, John Rowberry, Clay Caldwell and Lars Eighner are here represented by their most provocative writing. Michael Lowenthal, one of gay literature's new generation both edited this remarkable collection and provides the Introduction.
$12.95/233-7

GUILLERMO BOSCH

RAIN

An adult fairy tale, *Rain* takes place in a time when the mysteries of Eros are played out against a background of uncommon deprivation. The tale begins on the 1,537th day of drought—when one man comes to know the true depths of thirst. In a quest to sate his hunger for some knowledge of the wide world, he is taken through a series of extraordinary, unearthly encounters that promise to change not only his life, but the course of civilization around him. A remarkable debut novel. $12.95/232-9

MICHAEL LASSELL

THE HARD WAY

Lassell is a master of the necessary word. In an age of tepid and whining verse, his bawdy and bittersweet songs are like a plunge in cold champagne.

—*Paul Monette*

The first collection of renowned gay writer Michael Lassell's poetry, fiction and essays. Widely anthologized and a staple of gay literary and entertainment publications nationwide, Lassell is regarded as one of the most distinctive talents of his generation. As much a chronicle of post-Stonewall gay life as a compendium of a remarkable writer's work. $12.95/231-0

SAMUEL R. DELANY

THE MOTION OF LIGHT IN WATER

"A very moving, intensely fascinating literary biography from an extraordinary writer. Thoroughly admirable candor and luminous stylistic precision; the artist as a young man and a memorable picture of an age."

—*William Gibson*

The first unexpurgated American edition of award-winning author Samuel R. Delany's riveting autobiography covers the early years of one of science fiction's most important voices. Delany paints a vivid and compelling picture of New York's East Village in the early '60s—a time of unprecedented social transformation. Startling and revealing, *The Motion of Light in Water* traces the roots of one of America's most innovative writers. $12.95/133-0

RICHARD KASAK BOOKS

THE MAD MAN

For his thesis, graduate student John Marr researches the life and work of the brilliant Timothy Hasler: a philosopher whose career was cut tragically short over a decade earlier. Marr encounters numerous obstacles, as other researchers turn up evidence of Hasler's personal life that is deemed simply too unpleasant. Marr soon begins to believe that Hasler's death might hold some key to his own life as a gay man in the age of AIDS.

This new novel by Samuel R. Delany not only expands the parameters of what he has given us in the past, but fuses together two seemingly disparate genres of writing and comes up with something which is not comparable to any existing text of which I am aware.... What Delany has done here is take the ideas of Marquis de Sade one step further, by filtering extreme and obsessive sexual behavior through the sieve of post-modern experience....
—*Lambda Book Report*

Reads like a pornographic reflection of Peter Ackroyd's Chatterton *or A.S. Byatt's* Possession.... *Delany develops an insightful dichotomy between [his protagonist]'s two worlds: the one of cerebral philosophy and dry academia, the other of heedless, 'impersonal' obsessive sexual extremism. When these worlds finally collide ... the novel achieves a surprisingly satisfying resolution....*
—*Publishers Weekly*
$23.95/193-4

KATHLEEN K.

SWEET TALKERS

Here, for the first time, is the story behind the provocative advertisements and 970 prefixes. Kathleen K. opens up her diary for a rare peek at the day-to-day life of a phone sex operator—and reveals a number of secrets and surprises. Because far from being a sleazy, underground scam, the service Kathleen provides often speaks to the lives of its customers with a directness and compassion they receive nowhere else.
$12.95/192-6

LUCY TAYLOR

UNNATURAL ACTS

"*A topnotch collection...*" —*Science Fiction Chronicle*

A remarkable debut volume from a provocative writer. *Unnatural Acts* plunges deep into the dark side of the psyche, far past all pleasantries and prohibitions, and brings to life a disturbing vision of erotic horror. Unrelenting angels and hungry gods play with souls and bodies in Taylor's murky cosmos: where heaven and hell are merely differences of perspective; where redemption and damnation lie behind the same shocking acts. $12.95/181-0

ROBERT PATRICK

TEMPLE SLAVE

...you must read this book. It draws such a tragic, and, in a way, noble portrait of Mr. Buono: It leads the reader, almost against his will, into a deep sympathy with this strange man who tried to comfort, to encourage and to feed both the worthy and the worthless... It is impossible not to mourn for this man—impossible not to praise this book.
—Quentin Crisp

This is nothing less than the secret history of the most theatrical of theaters, the most bohemian of Americans and the most knowing of queens. Patrick writes with a lush and witty abandon, as if this departure from the crafting of plays has energized him. Temple Slave is also one of the best ways to learn what it was like to be fabulous, gay, theatrical and loved in a time at once more and less dangerous to gay life than our own. —Genre

Temple Slave tells the story of the Espresso Buono—the archetypal alternative performance space—and the talents who called it home. $12.95/191-8

RICHARD KASAK BOOKS

DAVID MELTZER
THE AGENCY TRILOGY

...'The Agency' is clearly Meltzer's paradigm of society; a mindless machine of which we are all 'agents' including those whom the machine supposedly serves.... —Norman Spinrad

With the Essex House edition of *The Agency* in 1968, the highly regarded poet David Meltzer took America on a trip into a hell of unbridled sexuality. The story of a supersecret, Orwellian sexual network, *The Agency* explored issues of erotic dominance and submission with an immediacy and frankness previously unheard of in American literature, as well as presented a vision of an America consumed and dehumanized by a lust for power. **$12.95/216-7**

SKIN TWO
THE BEST OF *SKIN TWO* Edited by Tim Woodward

For over a decade, *Skin Two* has served the international fetish community as a groundbreaking journal from the crossroads of sexuality, fashion, and art, *Skin Two* specializes in provocative, challenging essays by the finest writers working in the "radical sex" scene. Collected here are the articles and interviews that established the magazine's reputation. Including interviews with cult figures Tim Burton, Clive Barker and Jean Paul Gaultier. **$12.95/130-6**

CARO SOLES
MELTDOWN!
An Anthology of Erotic Science Fiction and Dark Fantasy for Gay Men

Editor Caro Soles has put together one of the most explosive, mind-bending collections of gay erotic writing ever published. *Meltdown!* contains the very best examples of this increasingly popular sub-genre: stories meant to shock and delight, to send a shiver down the spine and start a fire down below. An extraordinary volume, *Meltdown!* presents both new voices and provocative pieces by world-famous writers Edmund White and Samuel R. Delany.
$12.95/203-5

BIZARRE SEX
BIZARRE SEX AND OTHER CRIMES OF PASSION
Edited by Stan Tal

Stan Tal, editor of *Bizarre Sex*, Canada's boldest fiction publication, has culled the very best stories that have crossed his desk—and now unleashes them on the reading public in *Bizarre Sex and Other Crimes of Passion*. Over twenty small masterpieces of erotic shock make this one of the year's most unexpectedly alluring anthologies. Including such masters of erotic horror and fantasy as Edward Lee, Lucy Taylor and Nancy Kilpatrick, *Bizarre Sex and Other Crimes of Passion*, is a treasure-trove of arousing chills. **$12.95/213-2**

PAT CALIFIA
SENSUOUS MAGIC

A new classic, destined to grace the shelves of anyone interested in contemporary sexuality.
Sensuous Magic is clear, succinct and engaging even for the reader for whom S/M isn't the sexual behavior of choice.... Califia's prose is soothing, informative and non-judgmental—she both instructs her reader and explores the territory for them.... When she is writing about the dynamics of sex and the technical aspects of it, Califia is the Dr. Ruth of the alternative sexuality set.... —Lambda Book Report

Don't take a dangerous trip into the unknown—buy this book and know where you're going!—SKIN TWO **$12.95/131-4**

MC/VISA orders can be placed by calling our toll-free number
PHONE 800-375-2356 / FAX 212 986-7355
or mail the coupon below to:
MASQUERADE BOOKS
DEPT. U54AT, 801 2ND AVE., NY, NY 10017

BUY ANY FOUR BOOKS AND CHOOSE ONE ADDITIONAL BOOK, OF EQUAL OR LESSER VALUE, AS YOUR FREE GIFT.

QTY.	TITLE	NO.	PRICE
			FREE
			FREE

U54AT

	SUBTOTAL
	POSTAGE and HANDLING
We Never Sell, Give or Trade Any Customer's Name.	**TOTAL**

In the U.S., please add $1.50 for the first book and 75¢ for each additional book; in Canada, add $2.00 for the first book and $1.25 for each additional book. Foreign countries: add $4.00 for the first book and $2.00 for each additional book. No C.O.D. orders. Please make all checks payable to Masquerade Books. Payable in U.S. currency only. New York state residents add 8¼% sales tax. Please allow 4-6 weeks delivery.

NAME

ADDRESS

CITY_____ STATE _____ ZIP _____

TEL (   )

PAYMENT: ᴍ CHECK ᴍ MONEY ORDER ᴍ VISA ᴍ MC

CARD NO. _____ EXP. DATE _____